Judith Wade

Storm on Mermaid Island

I'll run as fast as I can to the village, close up Wild Violets, then run straight back. There's time...there must be time! Bonnie thought, and felt goose bumps race over her arms.

She didn't want to go out in the storm, but she couldn't let Wild Violets suffer another accident! If the front window got broken and the storm caused a lot of damage, Mrs. Caswell might give up on the store.

And if that happens, it will be my fault, Bonnie told herself bitterly.

She called her mother again and left a message on her voicemail saying where she was going, then opened the door and ran out into the rising wind.

Mermaid Dreams

by Judith Wade

Published by Riley Press, Eagle, Michigan

This book, including names, characters, places and events, is a work of fiction.

Book cover design by Colleen McCord.

Rileydog image by Tina Evans, Artist.

Some images copyright 2003
http://www.clipart.com

ISBN 0-9728958-3-3

Published in the United States of America by
Riley Press, P.O. Box 202, Eagle, MI 48822
http://rileypress.hypermart.net

To my daughter, who didn't mind wearing the wig, and my mother, who held the cape.

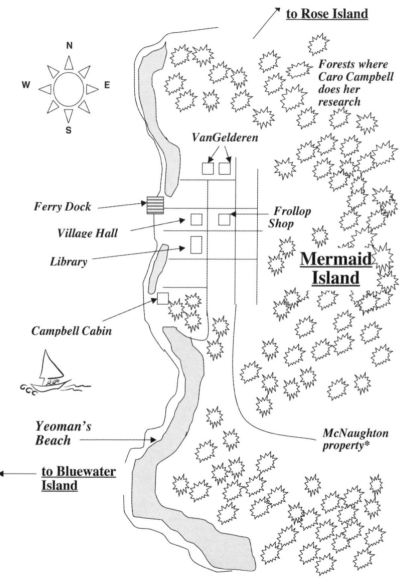

to Rose Island

N
W   E
S

Forests where
Caro Campbell
does her
research

VanGelderen

Ferry Dock

Frollop
Shop

Village Hall

Library

Mermaid
Island

Campbell Cabin

Yeoman's
Beach

McNaughton
property*

to Bluewater
Island

*see The Secret of Mermaid Island

Red sky at morning, sailors take warning;
Red sky at night, sailors' delight.
German proverb

1

When the rising sun turned the sky blood red for the third day in a row, Caro Campbell sighed and put her hiking boots back in the closet.

"I'm never going to get this research project done!" she groaned. "I wanted to get an early start out in the woods today, but it looks as if we're going to get another downpour!"

Bonnie smiled at her mother sympathetically and stared out at the horizon. She could see sparks of lightning flickering here and there in the churning thunderheads, and

Bluewater Island was barely visible off in the distance.

It was weird and scary, Bonnie thought, how the deep maroon color of the sunrise seemed to stain even the water a strange scarlet. It always signaled the coming of a storm.

"Those clouds are moving fast," commented Caro Campbell. "Oh well, I guess I'll just work at my computer today. I'll write about the plant specimens I've already found."

"I wonder why the water is so quiet just before it storms?" Bonnie mused. "It's almost as if it's waiting for something."

Bonnie's mother glanced at her, grinning.

"You have certainly grown to love the beach here," she said. "Mermaid Island stole my heart, too, when I was a girl. It's always been my special place."

Bonnie smiled in return and looked back out at the water, gazing at the reflection of the angry sky in the shifting waves. Her mother squeezed Bonnie's shoulder and then strode off to the study and her computer.

There's something different this summer, Bonnie thought. I've never seen the water like this. It's so still, so...well...watchful. As if it knows something is about to happen.

What was it like in the water when the trees bent in the wind and the waves rose, white crested and wild, to crash across the patient sand? Was it quiet deep beneath the surface, or did it surge and stir and tumble even there? How did the thunder sound, and what did the lightning look like?

If I lived under the water, would I be afraid of storms? wondered Bonnie.

A rumble of thunder made her glance up at the sky.

"Should I close the storm shutters?" she called to her mother.

The Campbells' little cabin had heavy shutters to protect its windows during high winds. All the buildings along the island's beaches had them, but Bonnie had rarely seen them closed until this summer when she and her mother returned to Mermaid Island.

Now it had been raining nearly every day for the past week, and several storms had struck with such fury that all along the beach shutters had been closed to protect windows from pebbles and branches hurled by the wind.

"I don't think we need to close the shutters this time," Caro Campbell answered from her study. "The weather service says today's storm won't be such a bad one. But I've got my computer running on battery in case there's lightning, and I unplugged the TV."

Good, thought Bonnie. I can watch out the window a little longer if the shutters are open.

Lately it seemed the water was all she could think about. As the waves' music sang her to sleep in the evening, she imagined them endlessly rocking her. She imagined them closing around her like a cool sheet on a hot summer night, imagined her hair floating as if it were weightless.

How would it feel to be surrounded by water, deep in Mermaid Island's blue, blue depths where no one could see?

Curling up in her chair, Bonnie pressed her face close to the window and began to search the crests of the waves for the extraordinary colors that were the island's special magic...greens and pinks, purples and bronzes. Most said the colors were a trick of Mermaid Island's dazzling sunshine, but Bonnie knew they hid a wonderful secret, a secret safely dwelling under the waves.

A mermaid lived there, and most marvelous of all was that Bonnie had seen her...talked with her.

Bonnie's heart gave a little leap. What was the mermaid doing now? Was she frightened? Or was she lying somewhere in the water watching the clouds roll in just as Bonnie was now?

Then the power flickered out, and the wind hit the cabin with a screech, rattling the door and flinging sand and dead leaves against the window panes. Caro Campbell emerged from her study, and Bonnie joined her at the kitchen table to wait until the storm passed.

Her mother sipped a glass of orange juice and shook her head.

"I've never seen so many storms on Mermaid Island!" she exclaimed. "Even during the summers I spent here as a little girl, I don't remember a storm season like this." She turned her glass on the table and frowned. "It sure is making my research more difficult," she added.

Bonnie suddenly shivered. Although she knew they were inside and protected, the sounds carried on wind were beginning to make her feel uneasy.

She listened more closely. Was that someone laughing? Or sobbing? Were those voices she heard, or was it simply the gusts swirling around their little cabin?

Bonnie fingered her grandmother's pearl hanging on its chain around her neck and felt tingles crawl up her arms. She rubbed them, trying to make the feeling go away, and glanced at her mother, who was reading quietly in the light from a flashlight. She appeared to notice nothing unusual.

Bonnie listened for a few more minutes and then put her head down on her arms, hoping to block out the sounds, but they still seemed to echo in her head. Bonnie shivered again.

An hour or so later, the cabin lights came back on and the island's bright sunshine began to push through the dark clouds, turning the water to glittering turquoise.

Grateful that the storm had finally passed, Bonnie ran to the window and looked south along the shoreline toward Yeoman's Beach. There she could see trees shedding raindrops that shone like diamonds in the early light. Now that the storm was over, the island looked like a fairyland, dazzling and magical.

Caro Campbell left on the ferry to do some research in the mainland library, and Bonnie dialed her friend, Bobbie, on the telephone.

As year-round Mermaid Island dwellers, Bobbie and her cousin, Moonie, were used to occasional bad weather. But this summer something strange was happening. Had her friends heard any odd sounds traveling on the wind?

As she listened to Bobbie's telephone ring, Bonnie imagined her friend scrambling across her upstairs bedroom, her red hair mussed and her green eyes sparkling. She had probably been listening to music or reading while the storm blew over the island.

"Hi Bonnie!" Bobbie's merry voice answered and then continued, "Let's go shopping today! My mom says the first new place in the 2588 Building...you know, where they're putting in those little shops...is moving in, and the lady who runs it is going to be there this afternoon. We can get a sneak preview! The store is called Wild Violets, and it's going to sell hand painted china! Besides, my mom says the building needs a welcoming committee, and I thought you and Moonie and I could be it! Help people move in and things. Do you want to?"

Bobbie sounded like her normal self, Bonnie thought, full of energy and excitement. Had the storm frightened her as it had Bonnie?

"Shopping sounds like fun," Bonnie answered, and then added, "It was a strange storm, wasn't it?"

"Strange?" questioned Bobbie. "It seemed pretty regular to me. But my granddad says Aunt Millie's coming to visit this summer, so we should look out."

"Aunt Millie?" echoed Bonnie, and Bobbie giggled.

"It's an old island saying," she replied. "Every hundred years supposedly Mermaid Island has a really, really bad storm. My granddad says you can tell it's Aunt Millie's summer by how your skin prickles before she arrives."

Bonnie's stomach gave a little jump, remembering how her arms had tingled.

Bobbie chattered on. "Aunt Millie supposedly comes after a whole bunch of little storms. The last really big storm here took out the boat dock and wrecked the roofs on a bunch of the beachfront houses."

"But why do they call the big storm Aunt Millie?" Bonnie asked.

"Oh, I don't know," said Bobbie carelessly. "It's an old legend or something…" Her voice died away.

Aunt Millie, Bonnie repeated to herself. The storms were definitely different this summer. Wilder and more frequent. Was there a really big one on its way?

"When did Aunt Millie come last?" Bonnie asked anxiously.

"Well, I guess about a hundred years ago," answered Bobbie, and Bonnie felt her heart sink.

Bobbie spoke into the silence. "There's probably no such thing as Aunt Millie," she said, hurrying to reassure Bonnie. "My granddad likes to tell tall tales. Besides, people know how to handle storms here. We'll be okay."

"I'm sure you're right," Bonnie replied, but she felt troubled all the same.

2

The 2588 Building was one of the oldest structures on Mermaid Island. It had belonged to a wealthy family at a time when the first big homes were being built by the beach, Bobbie explained to Bonnie.

Bonnie imagined how 2588 must have looked in the early days, its long boardwalk curving along the waterfront and its graceful porch smiling out at the waves.

But after the family who owned it died or moved away, the house became a hotel, then was finally abandoned, its windows boarded up and its paint peeling. For years it slowly decayed, and where once a crystal chandelier had welcomed visitors into the elegant entryway, cobwebs began to take over and hung in the corners like dusty lace. Mice nibbled at the carved doorframes and at the banister on the wide wooden stairway. The big glass windows grew dirty and shadowed.

"But then Mermaid Island's Historical Committee found the money to have 2588 restored," Bobbie added excitedly.

The Committee persuaded 2588's owner to rent rooms for beachfront shops that would attract tourists to Mermaid Island, as well as preserve the beautiful old house.

"And my mom's on the Historical Committee," Bobbie said proudly. "She helped with the fundraising!"

Bonnie thought 2588 was charming, with its fancy scrolling and pretty, freshly painted railings. It was perfect for little gift shops.

Bonnie, Bobbie and Moonie wandered along the boardwalk in front of 2588, admiring the sunshine on the new paint and looking for the sign for Wild Violets.

"There it is!" exclaimed Moonie, pointing, and they hurried up to the shop.

There were crisp flowered curtains hanging in the windows and Bonnie noticed the large garden box had been planted with roses.

Bobbie's mother, Polly VanGelderen, was standing in the doorway of Wild Violets and talking to someone inside. She smiled at the three friends and beckoned them over.

"Come meet Mrs. Caswell," she said, and stepped aside so the girls could enter the store.

A woman was standing behind the long wooden counter, smiling broadly. She wore a bright yellow sweater, and her hair was a shining gray, cut short and slightly curling on the ends. Her eyes were a merry, twinkling blue.

"Welcome to Wild Violets," she said, and then called over her shoulder, "Julie, come meet my first customers!"

The curtains to the back room parted, and a blonde-haired woman walked out. She had a smudge of dirt on her cheek and was wearing work gloves. Her jeans had a hole in one knee. She, too, had bright blue eyes, and a brilliant smile.

"This is my daughter, Julie," Mrs. Caswell said, and Polly introduced Bonnie and her friends.

"They've volunteered to help the new shops move in," added Bobbie's mother. "Maybe there are some things they can do for you?"

"Wonderful!" exclaimed Mrs. Caswell. "Perhaps you could help us begin setting up the display cases. They're arriving tomorrow."

"Why did you name your shop Wild Violets?" Moonie asked her.

Mrs. Caswell laughed, "Oh, it's a family thing. On May Day my daughters always used to bring me a bouquet of wild violets. So when I finally got my dream and opened this store, I thought I would use that name. Do you like it?"

"Oh yes!" answered Moonie, then continued eagerly, "Do you have any samples of your china?"

Polly called goodbye from the doorway, and Mrs. Caswell returned a friendly wave as she led the way to some boxes stacked in the corner.

"Now, let me see," she said, dragging over a stool.

Julie strode over quickly. "I'll help with that, Mama," she said. "You know you aren't allowed to lift heavy things!"

"My mother is recovering from surgery," Julie explained to Bonnie and her friends.

"She's really supposed to be resting, but she just didn't want to wait any longer to get the shop organized. I have to keep an eye on her, though. She works too hard!"

"I've waited years to open a china shop here on Mermaid Island, and I can't let a little surgery stop me!" declared Mrs. Caswell.

She winked at Bonnie and reached into the box Julie had brought down, drawing out a cup and saucer. Bonnie gasped.

The china was a bright white, and painted over it were pastels in sapphire, rose and jade, swirling and blending in a beautiful and complex pattern. Threaded among the colors were gleaming, hair-thin ribbons of gold, silver, bronze and copper glaze.

Bonnie held out her hands, and Mrs. Caswell set the cup gently into them.

"Did you paint this yourself?" Bonnie asked breathlessly.

"Yes, I did," answered Mrs. Caswell. She ran a gentle finger over the cup's gleaming surface. "I've got dish sets, vases, even a little tabletop, all in this design."

Bonnie stared at the cup in astonishment, and turned it from side to side to admire the shining surface and glowing paints. It was as if

Mrs. Caswell had painted the colors in Mermaid Island's waves onto her china!   Bonnie fell in love with the pattern instantly.

She set the cup carefully back into the box and went over to where Bobbie was admiring a little bowl painted with Mrs. Caswell's pattern.

"I'd like to buy one of these later on for my granddad," Bobbie said. "He's always picking up colored stones, and they would be beautiful in here."

"You girls are welcome at Wild Violets anytime," Mrs. Caswell replied. "I'm here in the shop every day during the week, and I have a little apartment in the village. But I like to spend Saturday nights and Sundays with Julie on the mainland. She's a lawyer, you know, with a busy job. She's taking time off to help me today."

Bonnie heard a cell phone ring from the back room, and Julie hurried to answer. Mrs. Caswell smiled.

"See what I mean?" she whispered. "That will be her office calling. As soon as she gets off the phone, we're going to go and pick up some cleaning supplies."

After looking around the store a little more, Bonnie and her friends bid Mrs. Caswell goodbye and went out onto the boardwalk, promising to return the next day to help her and Julie set up the new displays.

To Bonnie's surprise, Polly VanGelderen was standing nearby, hands on her hips, staring after a man who was walking quickly toward the main part of the village.

Polly's cheeks looked pink with anger. "That Fred Mahoney makes me so mad!" she exclaimed. "All he wants to do is tear things down all the time!"

"What's wrong, Aunt Polly?" asked Moonie.

"Oh, Fred didn't want this building restored. His company has a plan to buy the land all along here and build condos," snorted Polly. "He's telling everyone that 2588 won't stand up to the storms, especially the bad ones we're having this summer! He says nice new apartments would be better than these old homes."

Bonnie looked up at the stately old building. A lot of it still needed repairing, it was true, but where Wild Violets and other nearby shops were going in, 2588 looked beautiful, and strong, too.

"Do you think it might be damaged in the storms, Polly?" Bonnie asked anxiously, thinking of Mrs. Caswell and her dream of opening her china shop.

"No I don't," Polly answered firmly. "It's just Fred Mahoney making trouble! 2588 is a part of Mermaid Island's history! It has stood up to high winds before," Polly went on. "But Fred's even hired a consultant from the mainland to help him with his plan for the condos. We've got to get more shops moved into that building to pay the rent! Oh, I wish the Historical Committee could have bought 2588, but it was just too expensive! We were lucky to raise enough for the repairs!"

Shaking her head, Polly bid the girls farewell and started back toward the village.

Bonnie and Bobbie and Moonie exchanged dismayed glances.

"Well, that just makes my idea of a welcoming committee all the more important," declared Bobbie. "If we help people who are opening shops, maybe 2588 will fill quickly!"

Bonnie and Moonie nodded in agreement, and Moonie said eagerly, "We could carry things, or paint, or help set up, or even begin work on some of the other rooms that haven't been restored yet! It would be a great summer project!"

"Let's go have lunch and make plans," said Bonnie excitedly. "Where shall we go?"

"I vote for a sandwich and a frollop," said Bobbie, and Bonnie and Moonie quickly agreed.

Frollops were one of Mermaid Island's special treats…frozen pop with a dollop of ice cream. Bonnie always ate dozens of them with her friends during the Campbells' summers on Mermaid Island.

The threesome turned away from 2588 and began to walk toward the village, their minds busy with how they could help the new tenants. The beautiful building just needed some tender loving care, and the cluster of new gift shops would solve the problem.

Mr. Mahoney could just go build his condos on the mainland, Bonnie thought grumpily. She could hardly wait to come back and begin work for Mrs. Caswell.

3

That evening while Caro Campbell dozed over the newspaper, Bonnie slipped quietly out the screen door and strode down to the beach, enjoying the feel of the wind on her face and the sand between her bare toes.

Walking quickly along the shoreline, soon she arrived at an old tree, uprooted in the wind many years before, that stretched like a long bridge into the water. Bonnie paused and, rolling up her jacket like a cushion, she sat down on it in the warm sand—nearly dry now despite the rain that morning.

In the distance, the sun was sliding slowly out of sight and the waves were tipped golden in its last rays.

Bonnie stared thoughtfully at the water, her mind drifting once more to what it must be like to live where everything rippled and flowed and was constantly moving.

That was the mermaid's world. So different from Bonnie's, and yet...and yet...somehow Bonnie felt a pull toward the water that she had never felt before. Even at night, in her dreams, she felt the closeness of the mermaid and her people. What did it mean, this strange tugging she felt toward the waves?

Then she noticed a dark pool of indigo begin to spread in the water around the old tree, and she scrambled to her feet, shaking sand off her jacket.

The mermaid was here!

Soon the water was a riot of colors, glittering green and purple and magenta, and the mermaid rose slowly from the pool, her silver hair drifting gently around her white shoulders.

Bonnie noticed with surprise that the colors that always surrounded the mermaid looked even brighter tonight. Sparks seemed to twist in the water, golden and lavender, and her extraordinary eyes, now green, now shining turquoise, sparkled brightly.

She smiled in welcome and Bonnie greeted her eagerly, but then stood gazing at her, uncertain whether or not to tell the mermaid about how she had felt recently...of her dreams, and of the sounds in the storm.

"You look different somehow," Bonnie finally said, shyly. "Brighter, or more colorful..."

The mermaid smiled. "It is the summer of our celebration," she answered. "We prepare for it."

"Celebration?" Bonnie echoed.

The mermaid looked into the distance for a moment, then answered. "It is the time when the rains come. The rain makes the water strong, and my people strong as well. We believe that the celebration rains are coming, and we are happy."

She looked at Bonnie soberly. "But you must be very cautious," she said, her strange, rushing voice sighing past Bonnie's ears like waves over the cool sand. "These rains come only once in a very long while, and for your people it can be dangerous. The winds will be high, and the waves strong."

The big storm, Bonnie breathed to herself, that Bobbie and Moonie's granddad had warned about. The one the islanders called Aunt Millie.

"Some island people think a big storm is coming, too," Bonnie answered. "My friend says it's just a legend, but her granddad is making their family get ready."

"You must prepare also," said the mermaid. "It is a time of great rejoicing for my people, but you must take care. Especially those of you who live near the water."

Bonnie gazed at the mermaid without speaking for several moments.

"The wind sounds funny lately," she whispered at last. "And sometimes I think I hear someone calling. The waves or..." her voice died away.

She didn't know how to describe what she felt. It was as if the water had somehow crept into her head and was speaking to her there, whispering and singing, even when she slept.

The mermaid looked at her gravely. "Perhaps you sense the rains coming," she said. "The storm is still far away, but it is nearer every day. My people are beginning to gather. Some are coming from a long distance."

Bonnie felt a shiver slide up her arms. "How long do we have before it arrives?" she asked.

"I do not know," was the mermaid's answer. "It is still far away, but when it draws near, I shall warn you if I can." She smiled gently. "The wall between our worlds is very thin right now. I believe you feel this. It is nearly the time of the water."

Bonnie gazed at her. "The time of the water," she repeated, and then paused, thinking.

"You are drawing close to us," said the mermaid. "And I believe you will know when the storm approaches, just as we do."

When Bonnie finally bid the mermaid farewell and turned for home, she walked slowly along the beach, thinking hard.

Was she really closer to the mermaid's world? Would she at last begin to understand what the mermaid felt and how she lived? Bonnie felt a thrill of excitement.

But the storm, she reminded herself. Would she know, as the mermaid said she would, when it was going to arrive? In the meantime, what should she do?   And what about Mrs. Caswell and Julie, and Mrs. Caswell's new shop...her beautiful china? The older buildings were probably in the most danger.

Somehow she had to warn the people who lived on the beach about the coming storm without giving away the secret of the mermaid.

When Bonnie arrived back at the cabin, she found her mother sound asleep in her chair, her glasses askew and her newspaper on the floor.

Bonnie tiptoed past and settled in her place by the window, staring out at the water and wondering and worrying. After a while, her eyelids began to droop. But as she drifted, just short of sleep, she fancied she saw, dancing out in the water under the starlit Mermaid Island sky, the glint and flicker of distant lights moving here and there among the waves.

Bonnie straightened in her chair and gazed intently out the window.

Were the merpeople drawing together far out there in the water? Were they singing or laughing as they prepared for their celebration, or were they just gliding through the waves, their scales gleaming in the moonlight? And what of Bonnie and her friends. Were they in danger?

Troubled, Bonnie went to awaken her mother and then started upstairs for her little corner room.

4

"Has your grandfather said anything else about Aunt Millie?" Bonnie asked.

She and her two friends were strolling along the boardwalk toward the 2588 Building, sipping frollops along the way. Moonie stopped to pour some of her frozen treat into a cup for the little tan dog following at her heels. It was Carlotta Anastasia, Moonie's pug, and she had a brand new blue rhinestone collar, Moonie showed Bonnie and Bobbie proudly.

Carlotta Anastasia, snorting loudly, began to lick up the frollop with her pink tongue, and Bonnie laughed when she got ice cream on her nose.

"It's a good thing Mrs. Caswell likes dogs," Bobbie pointed out. "I don't think Carlotta Anastasia is going to be much help cleaning and painting at Wild Violets!"

"She'll be lots of help, won't you Carlotta Anastasia," Moonie crooned, kissing the little dog on the head, and Bobbie rolled her eyes.

Moonie grinned and looked over at Bonnie. "Yes, Granddad's still talking about Aunt Millie," she said. "He phoned my dad last night and made him buy caulking for two of our windows that he didn't think fit tightly enough."

"Are you getting ready, too?" Bonnie asked Bobbie.

"Oh, yes," Bobbie answered. "My mom even put a stone border around her flower beds to keep them from washing away in the rain."

"What other things do you need to do to prepare for Aunt Millie?" asked Bonnie anxiously, and Moonie shrugged.

"Well, you do what you would do for any big storm," she answered. "Make sure your shutters are good and tight. Stuff towels under your doors. Have candles and flashlights ready, and maybe a bucket if the roof leaks."

"Have your cell phone charged up," added Bobbie, "and make a list of emergency numbers. Unplug stuff in case there's lightning. Have a radio that runs on batteries."

"Have you done all those things?" Bonnie asked, and Moonie and Bobbie laughed in unison.

"Oh yes!" cried Bobbie. "Our granddad sees to that. He's been carrying on for weeks about Aunt Millie. But it's really just a legend, Bonnie. I don't think there's anything special about a particular storm."

Bonnie sighed. "If there really is a big storm coming, though, we should help people. Why don't we make it part of what we do at the 2588 Building? We could look around for things they should do to storm proof the shops."

Bobbie looked as if she wanted to tell Bonnie once again that Aunt Millie probably wasn't real, but she pressed her lips together and didn't say anymore, for which Bonnie was grateful.

She could not tell her friends about the warning she had received from the mermaid, but she was sure the mermaid was not mistaken. There was a big storm on the way. Bonnie had a sudden crawly feeling, and she rubbed her hands up and down her arms to make it go away.

The friends turned into the doorway of Wild Violets and were greeted warmly by Mrs. Caswell, who was behind her counter sorting a pile of papers. A box lay overturned on the floor and two stacks of plates were arranged in one of the new displays.

Bonnie spied a saucer teetering on the corner of a table and she gently pushed it so it wasn't in danger of tipping off.

Mrs. Caswell looked up distractedly from her paperwork.

"Oh, thank you!" she said, and then added. "I simply have to get organized. I don't seem to know where to start today. Julie has gone back to the mainland and I have so much to do! I have painting to finish, and these folders to put away and...oh!" Mrs. Caswell exclaimed, staring at the door.

Bonnie turned to see a man, accompanied by a well-dressed woman in a gray suit, enter the store. The man looked around and raised his eyebrows.

"Mr. Mahoney," whispered Bobbie to Bonnie.

"Oh!" Mrs. Caswell repeated, and then, "Hello!"

"How 'do, Mrs. Caswell," Mr. Mahoney greeted her. "This is Maria Reynolds," he introducd the woman at his side. "We're just walking through to see how things are going."

Ms. Reynolds must be the consultant working with Mr. Mahoney, Bonnie thought.

Mrs. Caswell looked slightly flustered, "We're doing fine, I guess," she answered. "I'm making some progress. But everything seems so disorganized. I don't remember leaving such a mess yesterday..."

"We're helping her," Bobbie spoke up quickly, and Mr. Mahoney frowned at her.

Ms. Reynolds walked over to the collection of plates and picked one up. She ran a polished fingernail over the painted design and smiled at Mrs. Caswell.

"These are very pretty," she said. "They would do well in one of the big department stores. Have you tried to get a contract with any of them?"

"Oh, no!" Mrs. Caswell said, looking surprised. "I would much rather just have my own little shop here on Mermaid Island. It's something I've always wanted, and..."

"It's a lot of work," Ms. Reynolds interrupted, still smiling broadly at Mrs. Caswell, and Mr. Mahoney chimed in.

"More money to be made in the big stores, too!"

"We're helping her," Moonie echoed her cousin, and again Mr. Mahoney frowned over at Bonnie and her friends.

"And of course," Mr. Mahoney continued, "it isn't certain 2588 will remain open. So much of it is in bad condition, isn't it? There's a lot to do to get it all repaired!"

Moonie nudged Bonnie with her elbow and scowled.

Ms. Reynolds laughed, a funny tinkling noise. "It's good you've got some little helpers!" she said, and Bonnie felt a twinge of anger.

Mrs. Caswell suddenly looked sad and unhappy, and she stared down at the papers in front of her as if she'd forgotten where they came from.

They were terrible to upset her, Bonnie thought fiercely.

Moonie and Bobbie glowered after Mr. Mahoney and Ms. Reynolds as they left the store, and Bonnie went over to stand near Mrs. Caswell.

"May we help with something?" Bonnie asked, and Mrs. Caswell looked up at her dully.

"Well, I was just going to sign these..." she said. She held up a gold fountain pen and several invoices.

"I'll address the envelopes," offered Bonnie, and sat down next to her at the counter. Mrs. Caswell thanked her, then turned back to the papers and began signing her name in beautiful, flowing script.

"What a pretty pen!" Bonnie exclaimed.

"It's my special one," Mrs. Caswell answered. "Julie gave it to me because she knows how I love a nice fountain pen. It's got the shop name on it, see? Oh, I do hope..." she broke off and gave a worried sigh.

Bonnie and Bobbie exchanged glances and Bobbie made a face in the direction Mr. Mahoney and Ms. Reynolds had gone.

Determined not to let Mrs. Caswell get discouraged, the friends dove into their projects with new energy.

While Bonnie helped with the paperwork, Bobbie and Moonie unpacked boxes, swept, and even painted a set of shelves. Later, Bobbie worked in the garden box outside and Bonnie and Moonie helped move boxes of papers into the tiny office to organize Mrs. Caswell's file cabinets.

Bonnie also began a storm emergency box, adding a flashlight and a pile of old towels. She showed Mrs. Caswell where the box was, and Mrs. Caswell promised to tell Julie, too. Tomorrow Bonnie would start going over the shop's shutters to make sure they were watertight.

By the end of the day, Bonnie was pleased to see the sparkle had returned to Mrs. Caswell's eye. She even knotted a rag and played fetch with Carlotta Anastasia, who had spent the afternoon sunning herself by the front door.

The foursome laughed merrily as Carlotta Anastasia skidded across the old wooden floor in search of her toy, and when Mrs. Caswell finally said it was time to go home, Bonnie left reluctantly. The day had been lots of fun, and somehow she hated to leave.

Mrs. Caswell was planning an open house for the village residents in less than two weeks, and would open for business shortly after that. There was still a lot of work to do. They would have to work for several more days just to get all the displays set up.

"I wish Mr. Mahoney would leave Mrs. Caswell alone!" Bonnie said angrily, as she and Moonie and Bobbie paused on the corner.

Moonie picked up Carlotta Anastasia, who gave a contented snort and then settled down in Moonie's arms, tired from playing.

Bobbie nodded in agreement. "He really upset Mrs. Caswell," she answered. "It's so mean! And all because he wants the building!"

"Well, he can't have it," said Moonie. "We'll make sure of that!"

Just then a rumble of thunder sounded in the distance and Bonnie jumped.

"Look at those clouds!" she exclaimed. "I'd better hurry home!"

"Call us when you get there!" yelled Bobbie as she and Moonie hurried off in the other direction.

Bonnie began to run down the beach path, but as thunder crackled again, she changed directions and instead sprinted toward home along the road.

Maybe I should have stayed in town! she thought suddenly, as an odd prickling sensation ran down her arms and back. The wind whipped her hair across her face, and Bonnie nearly stumbled. Running even faster, she rounded the last bend in the road and sighed with relief as she saw the cabin.

Throwing open the screen door, she fell inside just as hail began to fall.

Panting, Bonnie ran into the living room and slammed the windows closed. Then she unplugged the television as lightning speared across the sky and went to sit in the kitchen, worrying about her mother, who was working on the north side of the island on her plant inventory. She tried her cell phone, but there was no answer.

Then Bonnie heard Caro Campbell's car crunching to a halt on the gravel outside and her mom dove into the house through pouring rain, sheltering her laptop computer under her jacket.

"Well!" she exclaimed. "That storm surely came up fast!"

She unlaced her boots and removed her jacket, shaking it and placing it on a hook to dry, then ran her fingers through her hair until it stood up off her head in spikes.

"I am so glad to see you!" she exclaimed to Bonnie. "I didn't know if you'd stay in town or head for home, and that hail was pretty bad."

"I got here just before it started," Bonnie answered. "We heard the storm coming and left the village just in time."

Caro Campbell frowned at the rain slashing against the windows in their little living room.

"If it doesn't stop raining soon, we're all just going to float away!" she exclaimed.

"Do you think our cabin is pretty storm proof?" Bonnie asked. "Bobbie's granddad says this is the summer of the hundred-year storm."

"Does he really?" Bonnie's mother frowned thoughtfully. "Well, if he says so, he's probably right. He's lived on this island long enough to know 'most everything."

"He calls the storm 'Aunt Millie,'" Bonnie added.

Caro Campbell laughed. "Aunt Millie," she repeated. "It's a funny name, isn't it? Do you know where it comes from?"

"No," answered Bonnie. "What does it mean?"

Caro Campbell shook her head and smiled again, "Wow! This takes me back!" she exclaimed. "I first head this story when I was a little girl. Here's what I was told."

Mermaid Dreams

Caro Campbell sat down in one of the kitchen chairs and rested her chin in her hand, a distant smile on her face.

"Millicent Proctor lived here a long time ago," she said. "The Proctors had a huge family on the island. It was so big that her relatives just called her Aunt Millie, whether she was really their aunt or not, and pretty soon everyone was doing it. Aunt Millie loved storms. She always sat on her porch to watch them blow in off the water. Then one year...about a hundred years ago, I guess...there was a particularly bad storm season. Kind of like now."

"Aunt Millie seemed to sense there was a very bad storm coming. She tried to warn the islanders, but maybe people didn't take her seriously enough. She made sure her storm shutters were tight, and she stuffed rags around her doors to keep the water out. But here's the funny part. Her house had a big, big porch and a boardwalk. It was right on the beach, in fact. The storm came and went, and the wind did a lot of damage to the other homes all along the boardwalk, but Aunt Millie's house wasn't touched."

"People whispered that her house was protected somehow. They came to call that storm Millie's storm, and later just referred to it as 'Aunt Millie.'"

"Why was Aunt Millie's house protected?" asked Bonnie.

"I don't know," answered her mother. "No one does. It's just a funny old tale, and probably doesn't mean a thing. But it's an odd story, isn't it? Kind of gives me the shivers."

"Me too," agreed Bonnie, then added, "Is Mrs. Proctor's house still here?"

"Why, yes," said Caro Campbell. "In fact, it's that beautiful old home the Historical Committee is fixing up, where you girls are working. The 2588 Building."

5

The next few days seemed to speed by, as Bonnie, Bobbie, and Moonie helped Mrs. Caswell set her china into its displays and worked to get Wild Violets ready for its open house.

Bonnie went over the storm shutters inch by inch to make sure they would fasten tightly closed. Then she spent one afternoon caulking and painting every crack she could see in the old window frames along the front of 2588. It stormed twice, and water leaked along Wild Violets' door hinges, so Bonnie caulked there as well. She continued to add items to the emergency box, too--a little radio and some extra flashlight batteries.

Bobbie nursed Mrs. Caswell's rosebushes, and one began to bloom in big, fragrant yellow flowers. Mrs. Caswell cut one and put it in a rose bowl on the counter.

"Yellow roses are my favorite!" she announced excitedly. "I'm so glad they're starting to bloom, thanks to your help, Bobbie. They'll look very pretty for my open house!"

Bobbie went pink with pleasure, and Bonnie grinned at her. Polly VanGelderen was always planting something in her family's yard. It seemed Bobbie had her mother's way with flowers.

Julie came over and spent a long time moving boxes from her car into the shop. It was the rest of Mrs. Caswell's painted china inventory, she explained. She also brought a special finishing oil for the old wooden floors. She left the oil by the cleaning supplies to use the next day, and then disappeared into the office to work on the accounts while Moonie and Bobbie and Mrs. Caswell took Carlotta Anastasia to the beach for a stroll.

Bonnie was working to put together a bookcase, so she stayed behind at Wild Violets, trying to sort through the pieces and figure out which screws went with which shelf. For a while, all was quiet in the store, but suddenly Julie stuck her head out of the curtained office door, a worried expression on her face.

"Bonnie, will you come here a minute?" she called.

Bonnie put down the screwdriver and joined Julie in her mother's office. Julie was staring at a scattered pile of papers and folders.

"Didn't you girls organize all this the other day?" she asked, gesturing at the jumbled desk.

"I thought so," Bonnie answered, puzzled by the mess. Surely they'd put all the filing away?

Julie picked up a folder and then dropped it back on the desk. "These receipts are all mixed up and I can't find some of Mama's account information. She's had several mail-in orders we need to fill, but the paperwork is gone. I don't know where the customer addresses are!"

"Mrs. Caswell has been working back here a lot," Bonnie said worriedly. "Maybe she began a new folder?"

Julie frowned. "Maybe," she answered, then continued in a low voice. "My mom really shouldn't be working so hard. Sometimes she's so tired at night, she nearly falls asleep over her supper!"

Bonnie stared into Julie's concerned eyes and did not know what to say. Mrs. Caswell did seem to get tired, and she had complained about her office always being so disorganized, but no matter what Bonnie and Moonie and Bobbie did to try to help, it seemed it always got all mixed up again.

Strange things seemed to get lost, too. Yesterday it was her accounting book and her tax records. They found both items, but not until they had searched for several hours.

"I'm sorry," Bonnie said guiltily.

Julie smiled at her. "It isn't your fault," she replied. "But it isn't like my mother to be so scattered and untidy. I worry about her terribly! I wish she had her shop on the mainland so I could be closer to her, but it was her dream to open here on Mermaid Island."

"We'll help as best we can," Bonnie offered. "And I'll file all these papers again."

"No, I'll do it," Julie answered, and sighed. "There's just so much to do! And with the open house coming up, I feel as if we're running out of time!"

She turned to the desk and began stacking papers.

Bonnie parted the curtains to go back into the shop, and found to her distress that Bobbie, Moonie and Mrs. Caswell had returned. Mrs. Caswell was holding a panting Carlotta Anastasia in her arms and was stroking her absently, but her face had a sad expression.

Had she overheard Bonnie's conversation with Julie?

Feeling embarrassed and worried, Bonnie returned to the bookcase. The rest of the day passed quietly, and the tired group finally left for home in the mid-afternoon. Julie had a folder under her arm.

"I found those orders," she whispered to Bonnie. "They were just misfiled."

But how? Bonnie wondered. They were all put away just yesterday.

Bonnie stole a look at Mrs. Caswell, who had been very quiet after she had returned from walking with Bobbie and Moonie. Her forehead was furrowed, and her eyes distant, as if she were deep in thought.

She had overheard Bonnie's conversation with Julie, Bonnie was sure of it.

When they were ready to quit for the day, Mrs. Caswell locked the door to the shop and joined Bobbie and Moonie as they walked toward the village and home. Bonnie bid the group goodbye and started off toward the Campbells' cabin the other way down the beach path.

She paused by the old log and stared out at the water. That funny ripple ran up and down her arms again...an odd, cool feeling. The idea of the big storm still frightened Bonnie very much. She had stored emergency supplies at their cabin, and done all she could to prepare, but was it enough? She wished she could be like old Millie Proctor, with magic to protect her house.

To her surprise, she suddenly saw colors gathering in the water around the old log, and the familiar indigo pool, tinged with pinks and greens, began to spread among the branches. It was a strange time for the mermaid to show herself here...and dangerous for her too, as other islanders could be nearby.

Bonnie glanced around quickly, but the beach and the water were deserted. Most of the fishing boats must be up at north beach. She breathed a quick sigh of relief.

"I felt your sadness," the mermaid's voice slid around Bonnie. "You are afraid, or worried."

Bonnie gazed at the mermaid's lovely face. She never stopped marveling at what had happened to her here on the island. Although they had met many, many times, between visits it was still sometimes hard to believe that Bonnie had actually seen a mermaid. But here she was, right nearby, speaking to Bonnie, smiling at her. Had there ever been anyone so lucky?

"I have a lot I'm thinking about," Bonnie answered. "I have a new friend, a lady who has a store by the beach, and I'm worried about her. She's been sick, and I've been trying to help her, but I'm afraid she may not be well enough to do what she has always wanted to do."

The mermaid waited, drifting gently in the calmed water, her long turquoise tail glinting.

"And then there's the storm," Bonnie went on. "I'm helping my friend get ready, and I'm trying to tell everyone I can who has a home by the water, but people don't always understand. How long do we have?"

"No one can tell," the mermaid replied. "But we know it is coming. The water is waiting, too."

Waiting. Bonnie had felt it, had seen it as she watched out the window with her mother from the cabin.

"I am worried something will happen to my friends," Bonnie hurried on. "That the storm will damage something, or injure someone."

"You must do your best to prepare," the mermaid replied. "It's all you can do, but if you are careful, I believe all will be well."

Bonnie sighed. If only she knew what to expect...when the storm might come. What would it be like? But even the mermaid did not seem to know.

The mermaid slid slowly into the waves, and as the colors in the water spread and thinned, Bonnie's mind began to tumble again with thoughts about Aunt Millie.

Had Bonnie done enough to prepare Wild Violets for a bad storm? Would they have the shop ready to open only for the 2588 building to blow right down in the wind? How had Millicent Proctor kept the storm from damaging her beautiful home, so close to the water's edge?

Feeling uneasy, Bonnie turned and started back toward the village, hurrying along the beach path. She was going to check the entire outside of 2588 to be sure all the big old windows were protected. It wouldn't do to have Wild Violets stay dry but to have the building damaged in rooms where the renovations hadn't started yet.

Rounding the corner, Bonnie hurried along the boardwalk and turned at the sign for Wild Violets. Then she stopped in her tracks.

There was a light in the window! But Mrs. Caswell and Julie had both gone home. Who was in the store?

Cautiously, Bonnie crept up to the building and, standing with her back against the wall, turned her head to peer cautiously through the window. There was the bottle of oil for the floor, and one of the boxes Julie had moved earlier in the day. There was the bookcase Bonnie had worked on, and there...

Bonnie pulled her head quickly back and tried to think, breathing hard. Someone was moving around inside! Had there been a break-in?

There was a thump and Bonnie jumped. Holding her breath, slowly she peered back inside, her heart pounding.   The flowered curtains were partly blocking her vision, but someone was coming across the room...

Bonnie breathed a sigh of relief.

It was Mrs. Caswell! She was dragging a carton and clutching a handful of papers.

Soundlessly, Bonnie crept away. Mrs. Caswell must have left her little apartment and returned to get some more work done. She *had* heard Bonnie and Julie talking about how much there was to do. But Julie had said her mother shouldn't be moving heavy things...shouldn't be working so hard.

Worried and unhappy, Bonnie turned and trudged back along the beach path toward home.

6

The next day, Bonnie met Mrs. Caswell at the door to Wild Violets just as she was opening the shop for the day.

Bobbie and Moonie were strolling up from the direction of the village, Moonie holding Carlotta Anastasia in her arms.

"Julie's coming today," Mrs. Caswell said, beaming at Bonnie as she fit her key into lock.

She pushed the door open and stepped inside, then let out a shriek and threw out an arm to try gain her balance as her feet slipped out from under her.

Bonnie gasped and sprang forward, catching Mrs. Caswell by one elbow, but her feet slid as well, and for a moment Bonnie and Mrs. Caswell clutched wildly at each other, both of them sliding.

They crashed into the bookcase Bonnie had built, and a cup and saucer toppled off. Bonnie grabbed onto the top shelf, and soon both she and Mrs. Caswell had regained their balance.

Breathing hard, Bonnie stared down at the floor. What had they slipped on? The old wooden planks seemed to be covered with something dark and wet. Bonnie helped Mrs. Caswell over to the counter.

Her face was white, and she was trembling all over. She put one hand up to her brow.

Just then Bobbie and Moonie arrived at the door, and Bonnie shouted, "Don't come in! There's something slippery on the floor!"

The twosome halted in the doorway and Moonie peered inside. She handed Carlotta Anastasia to Bobbie and bent to pick something up. She held up a bottle--the finishing oil Julie had brought. It was empty.

"It looks like this tipped over," Moonie said.

Mrs. Caswell gasped, and the group stared at the floor in dismay. Where the oil had spilled, a dark, uneven stain spread across the wooden planks, stretching from just inside the door to halfway across the shop.

"Oh no!" Moonie cried.

"We need to soak it up somehow!" exclaimed Bobbie. "Paper towels, maybe? Or newspaper?"

"There's newspaper in the office," Mrs. Caswell said, and Bonnie hurried into the little room to fetch some, dodging the oil stain.

She looked with surprise at the scatter of folders and receipts on the desk, but said nothing. Grabbing a pile of newspapers, Bonnie returned to the main part of the store, and she and her friends spread the papers across the oil stain. Then Bobbie found a broom, and they swept up the chips of broken china.

The oil soaked up quickly, and within half an hour most of the really wet part had been cleared away. The dark stain was still very noticeable, however, and Mrs. Caswell stared at it in dismay.

"That oil is meant to go down evenly!" she cried. "Not in a big puddle. How could it have spilled? I don't know how we'll get it all up."

Bonnie, Bobbie, and Moonie looked at each other grimly, and Bonnie heard Carlotta Anastasia whimper anxiously from where Moonie had left her on the porch.

Mrs. Caswell had been here last night, Bonnie knew. It appeared she had been back in the office working on her paperwork, too. Could she have knocked over the oil bottle on her way out? Besides the mess on the wooden floor, it looked as if the account files were mixed up again.

Bonnie's heart felt heavy, and Mrs. Caswell was very quiet. She sat behind the counter looking through a book of invitations for her open house, but Bonnie could tell she wasn't really paying attention.

They took a lunch break, and Julie arrived just as Bonnie was clearing away the last of the sandwich wrappers and frollop cups.

"What happened?!" Julie gasped, as she spied the stain.

"Oh Julie!" Mrs. Caswell cried. "The finishing oil tipped over!"

Julie went over and took her mother's hands. "But how, Mama?" she asked. "It was capped."

Mrs. Caswell looked at her and shook her head sadly. "I don't know," she said. "When I left, it was fine, or at least I think it was. Oh, Julie. I feel so discouraged. Maybe this isn't going to work..."

Bonnie glanced at Mrs. Caswell, but again said nothing. Should she mention to Julie that her mother had come back to Wild Violets after the rest of them had left?

Julie went into to the office, and Bonnie heard her exclaim quietly at the scattered files.

Mrs. Caswell had begun to turn the pages again in the invitation book, and Bobbie and Moonie went to offer opinions on different styles of cards, so Bonnie tiptoed into the office where Julie was working.

She found Julie stuffing file folders back into the cabinet.

"I'm afraid the floor is wrecked," Bonnie said sadly.

"Well, it sure has a big stain, doesn't it," answered Julie. "I'm thinking about what do. We'll come up with something."

"Your mom nearly fell," whispered Bonnie. "I think it really scared her. The oil was everywhere, and it was really slippery."

Julie looked at her sharply. "How do you suppose it spilled?" she asked.

Bonnie shook her head. "I don't know. It was by the door when we left, and..."

"I'm pretty sure Mama is coming back in the evenings," Julie said, and Bonnie nodded.

"I wish she wouldn't work so hard," Julie continued, "But I can't stop her. She loves it so much here! She used to tell my sister and me story after story about Mermaid Island. She always dreamed of opening a shop along the beach. And it isn't like her to be so careless! I don't understand it!"

Bonnie looked at Julie in alarm.

"What do you think..." she began, but just then, Julie's cell phone rang and Julie pulled it from her pocket.

"Duty calls!" she said to Bonnie, sighing, and flipped it open to answer.

The group worked hard over the next few days to finish last-minute tasks and prepare Wild Violets for the open house. They put out the rest of Mrs. Caswell's china, polished her counter, cleaned all the old glass windows, swept cobwebs, and tended to the garden box. Julie came as often as she could—sometimes not arriving until late in the afternoon.

One day the files were all mixed up again, but Julie said nothing. She just quietly reorganized the little office, putting folders and receipts neatly back where they belonged. It stormed several times, and Bonnie was pleased to see that the big windows didn't leak once, despite the rain driving against the glass.

The storms were different, too. There was no scarlet sky to greet her in the morning, and she heard no funny noises on the wind. Bonnie began to relax slightly. Maybe the big storm was farther away than they had thought, or maybe it would even pass them by. But, the mermaid had said the rains made the water strong. What if the storm *did* pass by Mermaid Island? What would that mean for the mermaid and her people?

Bonnie sighed in frustration.

She gazed out the window often and longed to know more, understand more, about what life was like for the beings under the water. At night she went to bed feeling sad and worried, not knowing what to wish for.

The day before the open house, Bonnie caught Julie staring down at the big oil stain on the floor, a thoughtful expression on her face. She looked over at Bonnie.

"I've suddenly got an idea what to do with this!" she said excitedly, a smile spreading across her face. "Don't tell Mama. It'll be perfect!"

Bonnie looked at her curiously, but Julie held a finger up to her lips.

"You'll see!" she said, and grinned.

As Bonnie, Bobbie, and Moonie left the shop that afternoon, Bonnie saw Julie sketch something on a piece of paper and slip it into her pocket. She winked at Bonnie, her blue eyes sparkling.

"I'm coming back later," she whispered. "And tomorrow you'll all have a surprise!"

Wondering what Julie was planning, Bonnie wandered along the beach path toward home. When she reached the old log, she sat down in the warm sand and lifted her face to the waning sunshine. Lately she had seen the mermaid but briefly in the early evenings, and again she wondered what she and her people were doing now.

Mermaid Dreams

In the distance, clouds were beginning to gather on the horizon, and Bonnie saw a flicker of lightning. It would storm later, maybe during the night.

Where was Aunt Millie? Was she out there somewhere building up strength before heading for the island? Or was she not coming at all? The waves' colors twinkled, scarlet and lavender, in the late afternoon sunshine. Under those colors, the mermaid slid through the cool water, so very different from Bonnie and her world. Yet as time passed, Bonnie felt drawn ever closer to her and her people...thinking about them, dreaming about them.

Perhaps that's what happened when you let yourself believe the unbelievable, Bonnie thought idly. When you opened your mind to the impossible.

The rain clouds were drawing nearer, so Bonnie folded her legs under her and rose. Tomorrow would be a special day. Bonnie hoped the storm would stay away a little longer. Mrs. Caswell deserved a bit of good luck.

7

The morning of Mrs. Caswell's open house, Bonnie sat bolt up in her bed, awakened by such eerie sounds from the water that she clapped her hands over her ears. It was what she had heard before—calling and laughing and crooning—many voices now. Some of them were low, like men's voices, others sounded like women singing and humming, still others were like children's happy chatter.

Trembling, Bonnie scrambled from bed and ran downstairs to look outside at the scarlet streak of the sunrise spreading a red glow over the still water. Dark clouds were boiling along the horizon, flickering with lightning.

It's back, she thought. That strange red sky is back!

Bonnie heard a thump from outside and saw the storm shutters slamming closed over the living room window. She opened the door as her mother hurried back inside, trying to smooth her wind-tossed hair and rubbing her hands up and down her arms to warm them.

"Bonnie!" Caro Campbell exclaimed. "Did the thunder awaken you? There was one bolt that was so loud I swear I thought it was right overhead!"

"Thunder?" echoed Bonnie. "No, it was something else. It sounded like voices. Did you hear it? "

Her mother was looking at her oddly. "Voices?" she asked. "You must have been having a dream, honey, or maybe the wind?"

Bonnie put one hand to her forehead. The sounds had faded now, to just a distant murmuring. She sighed, and her mother's forehead crinkled in concern.

"Are you okay?" she asked, touching Bonnie's shoulder.

Bonnie tried to smile. "I think so," she managed. "A dream…you may be right."

But there had been something, Bonnie was certain. And it was not a dream. When she had first awakened, she thought it sounded scary, but now…perhaps it had been more like a big room of people, all talking at once, excited and laughing. Like a big family gathering for a holiday dinner.

"Sometimes the wind sounds crazy the way it blows 'round the cabin," Caro Campbell went on. "Maybe you should go lie down on the couch and see if you can get a little more rest."

Bonnie shook her ahead. "I'm not really sleepy anymore," she answered.

Then she thought dismally of the darkening sky.

"Oh dear," she moaned. "Mrs. Caswell's open house is today!"

Caro Campbell nodded in sympathy. "Let's go a little early," she said. "Maybe we can help her put down newspapers to catch the mud or something. And let's hope the storm isn't too bad!"

Bonnie rubbed her arms, which had begun to prickle, and went to sit with her mother. Was this it? Was this Aunt Millie?

Was the Campbells' little cabin strong enough? And what about 2588? Poor Mrs. Caswell, she groaned.

But again, the storm blew quickly across Mermaid Island, and by the time Bonnie and Caro Campbell arrived at 2588 that afternoon, the bright sun was even drying up some of the puddles. Although Bonnie was glad the rain wasn't going to spoil Mrs. Caswell's open house, her worries about Aunt Millie had returned. The clouds boiling along the horizon had frightened her deeply.

"Looks like there are already some cars here!" exclaimed Caro Campbell as she pulled the station wagon into the parking lot by 2588.

Bonnie dragged her thoughts away from the storm.

"I can't wait for you to meet Mrs. Caswell," Bonnie answered. "She loves roses, and she paints the most beautiful china!"

Bonnie thought her mother looked very pretty. She was dressed in a denim jumper embroidered with wildflowers, her short blonde hair was curled and she wore blue sandals on her feet. Bonnie, too, had dressed carefully for the open house, wearing a white sundress and her grandmother's pearl. She had even twisted her brown hair back in a painted clip, rather than its usual ponytail.

Julie met them at the door to the shop, smiling broadly.

"Welcome to Wild Violets!" she exclaimed. Then, "Well, what do you think?" she whispered to Bonnie.

Bonnie peeped around her and gasped with surprise.

On the old wooden floor, Julie had turned the big oil stain into a mermaid! The mermaid had a curled tail and long flowing hair, and her arms were outstretched, as if welcoming visitors to the shop.

"It's beautiful!" Bonnie cried. "How did you do it?"

"Just used more oil!" answered Julie. "It wasn't all that hard, really, once I had the idea in my head. Later we can put a finish over all of it to make it shiny."

Mrs. Caswell hurried up to them. She was wearing a yellow suit, and her cheeks were pink with excitement.

"Did you see Julie's artwork?" she exclaimed, and Bonnie nodded happily.

Bonnie introduced Mrs. Caswell to her mother and soon the twosome were deep in conversation about which roses were the most fragrant, and which ones had the longest lasting blooms.

Julie and Bonnie exchanged grins, and Julie whispered, "Don't tell anyone, but I don't have my mother's interest in flowers! I can't grow a thing!"

Bonnie laughed.

Bobbie and Moonie arrived a few minutes later with their two families, and soon village guests were streaming through the door of the shop.

Mr. Conner, the librarian, was there with his wife, and Mr. Davis, from the Frollop Shop, brought two big ice cream cakes for Mrs. Caswell's refreshment table.

"Come meet Granddad," urged Moonie.

Bonnie followed her over to where Moonie's parents were standing, and Moonie introduced her grandfather to Bonnie. He was a small man with short white hair that stood nearly straight up, and he wore a pair of thick glasses. Moonie's father helped him into a chair.

"Call me Pops," the old man said to Bonnie. "'Most everyone does!"

It was an opportunity to ask him about the storm, Bonnie thought suddenly, and she leaned down close to the old man.

"Pops, Bobbie and Moonie told me you think this will be the year of the hundred-year storm," she said.

"Sure will," Pops answered. "No doubt about it. She's comin' all right. Every hundred years. This is the year!"

"Aunt Millie?" asked Bonnie.

"Ha!" the old man laughed. "You've heard our island nickname for her. Aunt Millie's on her way. Yes, indeed."

"My mom told me about Mrs. Proctor," Bonnie answered. "This was her house."

"A fine old place," Pops replied, leaning back to look around. "A pleasure to see it getting fixed up. Town should never have let it fall to ruin. Our Polly took care of that."

"I tried to help storm proof it and make it ready for Aunt Millie," Bonnie went on anxiously. "I think it's okay."

"Sure it is," grunted Pops. "Just need to use some sense, is all. Lots of people 'round here don't seem to want to."

"This house didn't get damaged when a lot of other things did," said Bonnie rather timidly. "Do you think..."

"Humph," snorted Pops. "Don't listen to stories about Millie and her storms. She liked storms, all right. But she respected them. She respected everythin' natural. And Millie Proctor was no fool. She built her house to stand up to the winds. Built it strong, with the storms in mind. Nothin' magical. Just smart. She was a fine woman. A real fine woman."

"Did you know her?" Bonnie asked, surprised.

"Why sure, I did," answered Pops. "She died an old lady. Always loved a storm, she did. Kinda fittin' folks came to call that big ol' storm after her, too. Sometimes she had sort of a gruff way about her." Pops chuckled. "Didn't like foolish folk. No she didn't!" Pops chuckled and looked up at Bonnie, his old eyes twinkling.

"You and your mama will be just fine in your cabin. It's built strong, just like Millie Proctor's house. Aunt Millie would have liked you folks...yes, she would."

Bonnie blushed.

Just then Flip, Moonie's brother, and Pete, Moonie's little sister, came over from where they had been munching brownies at the dessert table, and Pete climbed onto Pops' lap.

Pops ruffled Pete's hair and asked, "What color are they today?"

Pete grinned for him, showing him her braces with new green and purple rubber bands.

"Very handsome!" exclaimed Pops, and gave a lock of her hair a gentle tug.

Flip pulled up a chair next to them.

"Want to see my new computer game?" he asked his grandfather. "It's a fishing one."

He handed the game to his granddad and they bent over it together.

"Can I catch me a whale with this?" Bonnie heard Pops ask.

"Bonnie!" Moonie whispered, and Bonnie turned to find her friend next to her. "Did you see who's here?"

Bonnie looked around the crowded room, noticing a line of people at the counter holding things they were purchasing, and Mrs. Caswell wrapping a plate in a piece of blue tissue paper.

"Over there," Moonie urged, looking toward the door, and Bonnie spied Mr. Mahoney and Ms. Reynolds standing in the doorway to the shop. Julie greeted them.

Ms. Reynolds had a bouquet of daisies in a pretty yellow vase, and she handed it to Julie with a smile. Then she looked down at Julie's mermaid and uttered a surprised exclamation.

"Why, how ever did you...How beautiful!" she cried. "Are you an artist?"

"Oh no," answered Julie. "I just took advantage of an unfortunate accident..."

Their voices were lost in the crowd.

"What is Mr. Mahoney doing hanging around here?" Moonie hissed.

Bonnie frowned. She looked over at Bobbie's mother, Polly, who was standing nearby as Mr. Mahoney and Ms. Reynolds joined a group of laughing, talking guests by the brownie tray.

Bonnie saw Mr. Mahoney take the elbow of a man in a red and yellow flowered tie and then gesture around the room. He was watching Mrs. Caswell closely as she lovingly packaged up a four-piece place setting of china for Mr. Davis.

Suddenly Bonnie saw Polly move away from Mr. Mahoney, a look of anger on her face. Bonnie nudged Moonie, and the two friends made their way through the crowd toward Polly VanGelderen.

Bonnie saw she looked grim and unhappy, and she was twisting the gold bracelet she wore around her wrist.

"What's wrong, Aunt Polly?" asked Moonie, and Polly shook her head.

"I was afraid of this," she said. "I just overheard Fred say he's offered to buy the building," Polly went on. "He's willing to pay an awful lot for it!"

"But it won't be sold, will it?" Bonnie asked anxiously.

Polly sighed. "The Historical Committee doesn't own 2588. We just paid to have it renovated. We can't prevent it being sold if the owner's losing money. He just has to give us our money back if he sells." She paused and looked around. "We must fill the rest of these rooms! If there are shops in them, and the folks are paying rent, then I think we're safe!"

Bobbie, who had joined the conversation with her mother, chimed in.

"Well, now that Wild Violets is open, we can help someone new that is renting a shop, can't we?" she asked.

Bonnie and Moonie both nodded eagerly, and Polly smiled. "You girls have been so nice to Mrs. Caswell," she said. "If you could pitch in on the next place, I'm sure the new tenant would really appreciate it."

"What kind of store is it?" Moonie asked.

"It's to be a book shop," answered Polly.

Bonnie and Moonie exchanged happy glances. They shared a deep love of books, and had spent many happy hours together reading on the beach. Bonnie imagined rows of bookcases and a corner with a big chair, near the window where the breeze could come in from the water.

"When can we get started?" asked Bobbie, grinning at her friends.

"The renter is coming in tomorrow for a while," said Polly. "I'll introduce you then."

Bonnie looked over to where Mr. Mahoney and Ms. Reynolds were chatting with the Wild Violets guests, then at Mrs. Caswell, who was laughing happily as she showed someone the little painted table.

Mr. Mahoney mustn't be allowed to ruin Mrs. Caswell's happiness, Bonnie thought fiercely.

8

The next morning, Bonnie met Moonie, Bobbie and Polly on the boardwalk by 2588.

The new bookstore was on the corner of the building, with two large sets of windows and a couple of wicker chairs set out on the big porch. A woman with her hair pulled back in a long braid looked up from where she was fastening a bird feeder onto a pole outside one of the windows.

A bird watching window! thought Bonnie. I like this place already.

"Angie Pratt, this is my daughter, Bobbie, and her friends, Bonnie and Moonie," Polly introduced them. "Angie is the new tenant. Her shop will be called the BookBin."

"We're here to help you get moved in," Moonie offered. "That is, if you'd like us to."

"They've been helping Mrs. Caswell in Wild Violets," Polly added. "But now Wild Violets' open house is over, they can begin working to get you set up. They're our welcoming committee."

"Wonderful!" exclaimed Angie, with a wide smile. "I'll take all the help I can get!" She flipped her braid over her shoulder. "Would you like to unpack some boxes?"

"Sure!" said Bobbie, and the three friends followed Angie inside.

Bonnie glanced around the little room and saw that Angie had sketched flowers and vines across the walls, with a big birdhouse drawing and several birds in the corner by the counter. It was an enchanting room.

"I'm going to paint those tomorrow," Angie commented, noticing Bonnie's interest in her pencil drawings.

"It will be beautiful," Bonnie answered, and felt her spirits lift.

If all the shops in 2588 were like Mrs. Caswell's and Angie Pratt's, then there would be lots of customers. It was a good sign.

Bonnie and her friends spent the next hour unpacking cartons and stacking books on the floor in various areas of the shop, according to Angie's instructions. The bookcases would arrive tomorrow, and then they could begin placing books into their spots on the shelves.

Julie stopped by the BookBin to say hello as she and Mrs. Caswell left to run errands and have lunch on the mainland. They praised Bonnie and her friends for their help in Wild Violets.

"We couldn't have pulled things together for our open house without them!" Mrs. Caswell declared, and Bonnie felt a surge of pride.

Bonnie watched Julie and Mrs. Caswell walk away toward the ferry dock, and a few moments later heard the door open again in Wild Violets.

Julie must have come back for something, Bonnie thought.

Julie explained that while on the mainland, she and her mother were going to buy a special finish for the shop floor that would seal it and cover Julie's beautiful mermaid art.

Bonnie could hardly wait to see the finished product.

It started to rain about half an hour later, and Bonnie closed the open windows in the BookBin, noticing as she did so several cracks she had missed in the caulking.

A job for tomorrow! she thought.

Then without warning what had at first seemed like a light shower turned into a downpour, rain blowing against the windows with heavy force and thundering onto the boardwalk.

"Have you ever seen such rain?" Angie shouted above the din.

"It's the rainy season," replied Bobbie loudly. "But we've had a lot more than usual this year, and storms, too!"

"You should be sure your storm shutters are closed during high winds," added Bonnie. "They need to be good and tight to protect your windows."

"Thanks for the warning," Angie said. "Where I'm from, it doesn't rain all that much. I've never used real shutters!"

Angie went to get a cup of coffee from her thermos, and Bonnie and her friends sat silently while the storm raged. A heavy gust of wind blew one of Angie's chairs over outside, and the bird feeder rattled on its post.

"Well!" exclaimed Angie, looking through the rain-washed window. "Maybe I need to get heavier chairs! I'll bring them in next time!"

When the rain passed, the three friends went for lunch at the Frollop Shop, and then wandered back along Main Street, window-shopping and sipping their frozen treats.

"Angie said I can bring Carlotta Anastasia tomorrow," said Moonie, and Bonnie smiled at her.

"She can organize the Pet section," giggled Bobbie, and her two friends joined in the laughter.

Just as the threesome rounded the corner onto the boardwalk, a door flew open up ahead and a woman's figure came stumbling out.

It was Julie.

"The most awful thing has happened!" she cried when she saw Bonnie and her friends. "Somehow we must have left a window open in the shop, and the storm did a lot of damage!"

"Oh no!" exclaimed Bonnie. "Can we help?"

"I'm going to buy some packages of paper towels," Julie answered. "There's water everywhere. We could use a mop, too!"

"We've got a mop and old towels at home," Bobbie said quickly. "Come on, Moonie. Let's go get them!"

"I'll go sit with Mrs. Caswell," Bonnie offered.

"Oh, thank you!" gasped Julie.

As Julie ran up the street, and Bobbie and Moonie hurried in the direction of their homes, Bonnie hastened up to the doorway of Wild Violets and paused in horror.

Water covered the floor where the rain had come in, and stacks of Mrs. Caswell's paperwork had apparently been blown out of the office to land in the puddles on the floor. Several sodden invoices were stuck against the wall where the wind had hurled them away from the window, and the pretty paper liners on many of the shelves were spotted with water. One of the displays had even blown over, and a china cup lay shattered on the floor.

Mrs. Caswell sat at the counter, her face in her hands.

"The storm did all this?!" Bonnie cried in surprise, and Mrs. Caswell looked up at her.

To her horror, Bonnie saw her eyes were filled with tears.

"Oh Bonnie!" she moaned. "I just don't think I can deal with this. My paperwork! All my tax records...my bills!"

Bonnie ran over to the counter and stared at the soaking wet papers scattered across the surface.

"Where did all this come from?" she asked, then added, "Is that ink?"

A dark spot stretched across the counter, staining some of the paperwork, as well as the wooden surface.

"My good fountain pen," Mrs. Caswell whispered. "I guess it leaked..."

Bonnie took a deep breath. "We must spread these papers out to dry before they stick together," she said quickly. "See, some of them aren't too wet. Let's begin separating the really soaked ones. Julie's coming with paper toweling. Maybe it isn't as bad as it looks," Bonnie tried to encourage Mrs. Caswell.

Mrs. Caswell rose from her chair and came to stand near Bonnie. "I hope you're right," she said, and bent to retrieve some of the drenched papers, but her hands were shaking so badly that Bonnie was alarmed.

"Wait!" she said quickly. "I'll clean it up. Can I get you some coffee?"

"That would be nice, dear," said Mrs. Caswell sadly. "I'm afraid I'm just not myself right now! I feel so upset!"

"It's the shock," Bonnie told her, praying she was right. "You'll feel better soon."

She helped Mrs. Caswell back into her chair and brought her some coffee from Angie Pratt's thermos, and Angie herself came back to help, carrying a broom and dustpan. Then the others arrived, too, and the store began bustling with activity.

Bobbie and Moonie mopped up water, Angie gently removed the sodden shelf papers from Mrs. Caswell's displays, and Mrs. Caswell went to pick up the broken cup and sweep up the chips.

Bonnie watched her warily, but she seemed to be recovering from her weakness and Bonnie saw with relief that her hands were steady. Bonnie and Julie began sorting papers and setting them to dry on paper towels that Bonnie had lain across the counter.

Suddenly Bonnie saw Julie lean over and stare at the ink stain, her eyes narrowed. Then she gazed at the door with a look of such fury that Bonnie was startled.

"What's the matter, Julie?" she asked timidly, and Julie beckoned to Bonnie, calling her around behind the counter.

She pointed to the ink and said quietly, "Take a good look at that stain, Bonnie."

Bonnie stared down at the spot and then answered, "Your mom's pen…"

"But it isn't!" hissed Julie angrily. "My mom's fountain pen is blue, not black. This ink isn't from her pen!"

"But…" began Bonnie, and Julie held a finger quickly up to her lips, cautioning Bonnie to keep her voice low.

"What do you mean?" Bonnie whispered.

"We didn't leave that window open," Julie said grimly. "I'm sure we didn't."

"I heard you come back…" Bonnie began. "Maybe you didn't notice…" but Julie interrupted her.

"Come back?" she demanded. "From lunch?"

"No, I mean before lunch," Bonnie replied. "Just after you left, I heard the door open again."

"But, we didn't come back," Julie said in a low voice.   Her blue eyes glittered. "Someone's been in here," she said.

9

"What?" Bonnie squeaked. "What do you mean?"

"Someone helped cause this," Julie answered grimly. "It wasn't all done by the storm."

"Are you sure?" Bonnie gasped. "But how? And why?"

Julie ducked through the curtains into Mrs. Caswell's office, holding her finger to her lips, and beckoned for Bonnie to follow.

"Shh," Julie whispered, "I don't want to alarm Mama."

Then she went on, "I was suspicious when the other things happened," she said. "Like that oil bottle. How did it get opened? And then all those times when Mama's office was messed up. Little things, but something's not right. She may be still recovering from her surgery, but she's very careful with her files and records."

"She was coming here alone and trying to work in the evenings," said Bonnie timidly. "Maybe she got tired, or...?"

"I know she's been tired," answered Julie firmly. "But she wouldn't leave her things that way. I know her, Bonnie. It's the last thing she would do."

Bonnie stared into Julie's worried eyes, her heart pounding.

"Besides," Julie went on. "Where did the ink stain on the counter come from? Mama's fountain pen was lying there, it's true, and it was uncapped. But why? Mama never leaves it uncapped. And even if she did, it's the wrong color ink. Someone spilled it deliberately. You heard them come into the store after we left."

Bonnie stared at Julie in horror.

Julie went on angrily. "Wild Violets is my mother's dream. I will not let anyone destroy it!"

Outside in the shop, Angie and Mrs. Caswell were talking in low voices, and Bonnie could hear Bobbie teasing her cousin.

Bonnie's mind was whirling. "What shall we do?" she asked Julie.

Julie wrinkled her brow. "I need to think," she answered, pressing a hand to her forehead. "Please don't tell my mother about my suspicions right now...not until I come up with a plan for what to do next."

"Bobbie and Moonie and I can help," offered Bonnie.

"Okay," answered Julie. "But no one is allowed to take any risks. You leave things to me for now, all right? We don't know that there's any danger. But we don't know there isn't, either."

Bonnie felt a chill slide up her arms. Danger? She hadn't thought about that.

But someone was breaking into Wild Violets, and whoever it was did not mean Wild Violets well.

"Okay," Bonnie whispered. "We'll be careful."

Julie stared thoughtfully down at the desk. "We need to set a trap of some sort. But what might it be?"

There was a sudden burst of laughter from out in the shop, and Julie smiled at Bonnie.

"It sounds as if folks are cheering up," she said in a brighter tone of voice. "Let's go help them before they think we're hiding back here to get away from the work! I'll let you know when I come up with a plan."

Bonnie gave Julie a small smile in return, and followed her out to the main part of the store.

For the next two hours, the group cleaned and picked up, sorted and swept puddled water out onto the boardwalk. By the time they closed and locked the door behind them, Wild Violets looked almost completely normal again, except for the papers drying along the counter. Tomorrow Julie would help Mrs. Caswell sort them into folders and put them away.

To everyone's relief, most of the ink stained invoices were copies and not originals, and many were only spoiled on the corners anyway. But the pretty counter had an ugly spot in one place where the ink had colored the wood.

Mrs. Caswell wrung her hands, but Julie just looked at it and shrugged.

"Looks like some more mermaid art for me!" she joked, and the others laughed.

They left Angie at the BookBin, and Bobbie promised they would return the next day. Then Bonnie and her friends waved goodbye to Mrs. Caswell and Julie.

The three girls lingered on the corner by 2588 as they watched Julie and her mother drive away, and then Bonnie turned breathlessly to Bobbie and Moonie.

"You guys, Julie and I don't think the storm made all that mess!" she exclaimed.

"I don't either," answered Moonie. "The wind blew really hard and everything, but it just didn't look right."

Bobbie nodded in agreement.

Bonnie told her friends about her conversation with Julie in the office.

"I knew it!" exclaimed Bobbie when Bonnie had finished. "You'd have to be really careless to keep leaving paperwork out all the time, and I didn't think Mrs. Caswell would do that. She kept putting it away, not taking it out! And that finish oil for the floor. How did it get spilled unless someone did it deliberately?"

"That's right," answered Bonnie grimly. "And whoever it is knows how to get in, or else they have a key."

"Well, we can keep an eye on the store for Julie," Moonie said. "We'll be at the BookBin during the days and we can keep watch for anything suspicious."

"Julie's plotting something," said Bonnie. "She wants to stop the person who is wrecking Wild Violets."

"Oh! This is just like a TV show!" cried Bobbie excitedly.

"Maybe she'll buy a burglar alarm," suggested Moonie.

"Maybe…" answered Bonnie. "I don't know what she is going to do. She said she wanted to think about it."

"She won't let anyone drive her mother out," said Moonie, and Bobbie and Bonnie nodded in agreement.

"I'd better go home," said Bonnie at last. "We're supposed to be barbecuing when my mom gets back from the woods."

"Okay," answered Bobbie. "Shall we meet around ten o'clock tomorrow?"

"Great," said Bonnie, and waved farewell to her friends.

She started along the boardwalk toward home, but suddenly she stopped. Something seemed to be pulling her toward the beach path...calling her, telling her...something. What?

Bonnie stared intently in the direction of the water. Everything looked as it always did. The beautiful Mermaid Island sun was glinting on the tumbling waves. Several couples strolled slowly down the sand toward the ferry dock, and a dog barked shrilly, chasing a stick down the sand and bringing it back so a little boy could throw it for him again.

But the pull toward the water was so strong that Bonnie turned and began to jog hurriedly back toward the beach path, staring out at the waves as the feeling became even stronger. Something or someone seemed to be calling to her. And it was coming from the direction of the old log!

Quickly, Bonnie made her way through the tall grass and onto the beach.

The sun was dropping low in the sky— the time of day when the mermaid often ventured out.

Was it the mermaid? Bonnie thought excitedly. Was she waiting, hoping to talk with Bonnie?

Mermaid Dreams

Bonnie ran down the beach, her sneakers digging into the sand and her heart pounding. Rounding a bend, she paused by the log where she and the mermaid had met so often, and shaded her eyes to gaze out at the water.

Red glints sparkled among the restless waves, and around the trunk of the fallen tree a silvery blue began to darken into indigo.

It *was* the mermaid calling! Bonnie thought excitedly. But how had she done it?

She ran to the water's edge and stared out at the pool around the log. The waves there were growing calm, and the dark blue was spreading wider and wider. Her heart thumping, Bonnie waited.

Then the mermaid's startlingly white face arose from the shining pool, and her welcoming smile sent a glow of warmth through Bonnie.

The colors in the waves were brilliant today, and the mermaid's silver hair seemed to glow nearly sapphire where it met the water.

"You called me!" Bonnie exclaimed.

The mermaid nodded, and Bonnie saw her turquoise tail flash beneath the surface of the water.

"I thought perhaps you would hear me," the mermaid said in her strange voice. "Our worlds are drawing very close together now."

"I am so happy!" cried Bonnie. "I have wanted this so much…to be able to be closer to you and your people!"

"It is a special time," answered the mermaid, but then her face grew sober. She drifted slightly in the calm water, and Bonnie saw her tail move restlessly. "I called to you to warn you," the mermaid went on.

"Of the storm?" Bonnie asked worriedly.

The mermaid nodded. "It draws very close now. It is no more than three of your days away, and perhaps not even that many."

"I have done as you said," Bonnie told the mermaid. "The house where I live is strong, and will hold up to the winds. I have told my friends, and helped them get ready, too."

"That is well," said the mermaid. "We, too, are preparing. My people are all gathered now. The celebration will begin soon."

"I wish I could join in your celebration!" sighed Bonnie. "I can only imagine what it is like!"

The mermaid cocked her head, drifting in the water. "Perhaps you will know of it, I do not know. You have a special gift that makes you different from others like you. You see us, you speak with us, and now you know when we call to you. But you must take no chances with the coming storm!"

"I won't," promised Bonnie. "We will be safe."

She watched as the mermaid raised a white hand in farewell. Then her body slipped into the waves and soon the colors were drifting slowly away, turning pale and nearly disappearing in the gathering shadows.

Bonnie turned for home, her mind racing. Someone was doing his or her best to upset Mrs. Caswell and perhaps to drive her away. And now the big storm was approaching. There was much to think about and to do.

10

The next morning, Bonnie stared anxiously out at the sky, but saw nothing unusual there—no dark clouds, no lightning flickering on the horizon. The weather forecast said a beautiful day was likely. Apparently the storm would not come today.

When Bonnie, Bobbie and Moonie arrived at 2588, Bonnie saw Julie carrying a large box into Wild Violets. A few minutes later, she emerged and went back to her car, this time returning with a bucket and a tool kit.

Promising Angie they would be back in a moment, the three friends ran over to Wild

Violets and burst inside. Julie was dragging a ladder out of the office and chuckling under her breath.

"What are you doing?" Bonnie asked, and Julie began to laugh.

"I'm doing several things," she answered, and smiled at the puzzled look on Bonnie's face.

"Are you painting a mermaid on the ink stain?" Bobbie asked, and Julie pointed to a box on the counter.

"That's what those brushes and paints are for," she said. "I'll get at that in a minute, but first I want to show you something."

Julie pulled the ladder the rest of the way over to the door and climbed it while Bonnie, Bobbie, and Moonie gathered around, staring up at her.

"See this bracket?" Julie asked, holding up something that looked like a hinge. "I'm going to fasten it on here," she went on. "And then...Bonnie, hand me that bucket, will you?"

Bonnie ran over and held up a small plastic bucket so Julie could grab the handle.

Julie set the bucket on the bracket, and then said, "Here's how it works. When we leave at night, we fill the bucket with water and set it up here. Then we pull this little string through the door. See? It's fishing line and it's nearly invisible. If you unhook it before you come inside, it'll flip up the other side of the bracket and hold the bucket in place. But if you don't…" Julie grinned down at the three friends and tugged the string.

The bucket tipped off the bracket and Moonie caught it as it tumbled down. Julie burst into laughter.

"Splash!" she cried, and Bonnie and Bobbie began to laugh along with her.

"That's right," said Julie. "Someone gets a bucket of water dumped on their head before they even get inside! It won't actually catch anyone, but it'll let them know we're on to them."

"It's perfect!" crowed Bobbie.

"Where will you hide the string?" she asked, and Julie showed her how she would fasten it just inside the doorframe.

"No one will notice that," said Bonnie.

"I don't think so either," said Julie. "But you guys need to remember…don't forget to pull the string before you come in, or you're going to get very, very wet!"

Julie took a screwdriver and a couple of screws out of her back pocket and began to fasten the bracket to the wall.

"Where's your mom?" asked Bonnie.

"We're going to take the day off, and she's going to my house tonight," answered Julie. "There's been a lot of excitement this week, and she needs to rest up for Wild Violets' opening day. I'm just going to finish this up, do the painting on the counter, put away a few things, and then head for the mainland. If you see anything, though, please call me. You have my cell number."

"Okay," Bonnie promised.

"I'll drop by a little later with a key," Julie added, and then turned to her work.

Bonnie and her friends were still laughing when they arrived at Angie's, and Angie looked up from where she was sorting a box of magazines.

"What's so funny?" she asked.

Bonnie glanced at the others, and then answered, "Oh nothing. Just Julie joking around, that's all."

Bonnie was sure Angie wouldn't tell anyone about the bucket trap, but just in case, it was best to keep the plan to themselves.

Moonie had left Carlotta Anastasia tied to the birdhouse post outside the BookBin, so she went and fetched her, and then the three friends began to help Angie organize her books into the new bookcases.

"Put the pet books over here!" Angie called, and Carlotta Anastasia trotted over to stare at the shelf where Angie was pointing.

"See, Carlotta Anastasia even approves!" said Angie, and Moonie laughed.

It was a happy, fun-filled afternoon as Bonnie, Bobbie and Moonie began to see the big room Angie had painted so carefully transformed into a cozy bookstore. Rows of hardbounds lined the walls, while the inside shelves held paperback books and magazines, and even a little display of pens, bookmarks, and writing journals that Angie called the "Artist's Corner."

Angie pulled two big chairs and a table over near the window by the birdfeeder, and then motioned to the corner where there was a small cabinet.

"I need to paint that," she said. "And then that's where my coffee-maker goes!"

"It's perfect, Angie," Bonnie said sincerely.

The BookBin was going to draw lots of customers, Bonnie thought happily.

Soon 2588 would be filled with stores just like Wild Violets and the BookBin, and then everything would be well with the old house.

Bonnie gave a contented sigh.

"I'm going to head home early today," said Angie, and walking outside she swung the storm shutters closed. "I just want to make sure," she added, and smiled at Bonnie. "I won't be here tomorrow, and I want everything safe while I'm gone. After what happened in Wild Violets..."

Bonnie saw Bobbie exchange glances with Moonie. Did Angie suspect that the flood in Mrs. Caswell's store hadn't been an accident? If so, she had said nothing. The sooner they figured out who was doing it the better, Bonnie thought worriedly.

And the storm...

Tomorrow night when they closed up at Wild Violets, Bonnie would make sure the shutters were tightly shut and rags were under the doors. The mermaid had said three days, but it was better to be safe. Bonnie felt a thrill up her back and looked nervously out at the horizon.

As she and Bobbie and Moonie started along the boardwalk, she glanced around her to be sure no one was watching and then did a quick check that the fishing string was in place in the doorway to Wild Violets. There it was, tucked securely against the doorframe, nearly invisible. Now to see what happened!

Bonnie bid her friends farewell, and headed down to the beach path. She paused briefly at the old log and stared out at the water, but the colors were pale this time...hardly noticeable, unless she looked carefully.

There was no sign of the mermaid, no gentle calling to tell her the mermaid wanted her, no indigo stain drifting around the old tree. Where was she? Were she and her people gathered somewhere out in the water? What were they doing?

The wind whipped Bonnie's hair across her face, and she pushed it away. Were the whitecaps a little taller than normal? she thought suddenly. Did the surf look a little stronger, a little higher? A funny feeling was starting to grow in Bonnie's mind, and she almost fancied she could hear the voices again...laughing and calling. What was it?

Worried, Bonnie turned and hurried home. Inside, she could hear her mother muttering as she worked away on her laptop.

Bonnie flipped on the TV in the living room and then stuck her head into her mother's study.

"Hi!" she called softly.

Her mother jumped slightly and then turned around in her chair.

"Hi, Bonnie," she answered. "I didn't hear you come in!"

She ran a distracted hand through her tousled blonde hair and then made a face.

"Oh, I'm having problems here," she said. "Somehow I've lost some of the data I got at the mainland library. I'm going to have to go back tomorrow and look it up again."

"Tomorrow?" Bonnie echoed. She felt uneasy. How close was the storm?

"Just for a few hours," Caro Campbell replied, and then sighed. "I don't want to go, but there's a lot to do, and I'm a little behind..."

Bonnie turned and look at the television. The weather report would be on soon.

"What's the matter?" her mother asked.

"It's the storm," Bonnie answered. "People are talking about it, and I...well...I think it may be here soon. The wind is funny...different somehow. I felt it when I walked home."

"Really?" Caro Campbell stood up and looked out the window of her study at the water.

She gazed out at the waves for several minutes and then shook her head. "I can't see anything unusual, but if it's storming in the morning I won't go, okay? And if it isn't, I'll still make it a very quick trip. Just to get a few pieces of information, and then if the storm does come I'll have what I need to work here with my laptop on battery."

Bonnie turned back to the living room. "Can we see what the weather says?" she asked.

She sat down on the couch, and her mother joined her, smiling at her. They watched the end of the news, then the sports, and then the weather forecast came on.

But there seemed to be nothing of concern. There was a large storm over the water, but it was not moving inland. Thunderstorms were predicted for Mermaid Island, but that had been true the entire summer. There was a small boat warning due to possible high winds by tomorrow afternoon.

Caro Campbell looked over at Bonnie and shrugged. "Doesn't look like anything to be worried about yet," she commented. "But we'll check again in the morning."

"Okay," answered Bonnie.

Her mother went back to her study, and Bonnie wandered upstairs to change for supper. Despite what the weather forecast said, Bonnie still felt unsettled. The mermaid had said three days, but perhaps two. Was the storm coming earlier?

How Bonnie wished she could talk to the mermaid now. Sighing, she sat down on her bed.

11

The next morning when Bonnie awoke, she was startled to see a deep red sunrise staining the sky as far as she could see in both directions.

Caro Campbell joined Bonnie at the window. "That's an amazing sky, isn't it?" she commented. "I don't see any clouds right now, but the weather service says it'll be storming by this afternoon."

"I really wish you wouldn't go, Mom," said Bonnie, watching her mother pull a jacket out of the closet.

"But Bonnie," her mother protested, "It's quiet right now and I promise I'll be back by noon!"

Caro Campbell kissed her daughter, shouldered her backpack, and walked out to the station wagon, glancing once more up at the sky.

She opened the driver's side door, and then called to Bonnie, "And if *anything* looks as if it's going to change, I'll come back right away. You don't want me cooped up in the house without my work, do you?" she teased, and Bonnie grinned, imagining her mother pacing and fussing.

She was happiest when she was out in the woods, but next best was working at her database, sorting and classifying her list of plants.

So Bonnie waved goodbye and went into the cabin. Restlessly, she walked to the window and stared out at the water. The waves looked almost normal, but perhaps their white caps were just a bit taller, and twisting somehow, as if some invisible force was pulling them.

Bonnie ran back to the cabin door, hoping to call to her mother, but the car was out of sight.

Troubled, she telephoned Moonie, whose line was busy, and then Bobbie.

Bobbie answered rather breathlessly. "My granddad is over, and he's positive one of those storms coming in this afternoon is going to be the big one, Bonnie!" she exclaimed.

Bonnie's stomach lurched.

"My dad and Uncle Bart are out fastening our storm shutters closed, and stuffing rags under the garage doors! I was going to call you in a minute and tell you to do the same! Everyone down our street is getting prepared, too. Oh Bonnie, I'm sort of scared!"

Why, oh why, didn't I call Bobbie before Mom left? thought Bonnie desperately. I knew something was happening! I just knew it!

"Bonnie?!" Bobbie cried, and Bonnie realized she'd let the phone line go silent.

"I'm here," she answered, trying to sound calm. "I'm just worried because my mom's gone to the mainland to the library, but she'll be back soon. I'll go close our storm shutters and get everything ready!"

"Okay," answered Bobbie, then, "I'd better go. Call us if you need any help. I'm going down to help Mr. Davis put up the shutters over the window on the Frollop Shop."

Mermaid Dreams

Bonnie hung up, and ran to dial her mother's cell phone.

She's probably still on the ferry, thought Bonnie as she heard the recorded message saying her mother's phone was turned off.

Restlessly, Bonnie went back to the window and stared out at the water.

She gripped the windowsill. Was it her imagination, or was there an odd gray haze on the horizon?

Bonnie stared at it. One moment, the gray seemed to be growing and spreading; the next moment it seemed not to be there at all.

Shaken, Bonnie went into the kitchen and pulled out the drawer where she her mother kept their flashlights. She put two of them on the table, along with a package of extra batteries. Then she set the portable radio on the table as well, filled two large jugs of water and put them in the refrigerator, unplugged the television and the rest of the entertainment center, and her mother's computer.

The phone rang. It was Moonie.

"Do you want to come over?" she asked Bonnie.

"No," answered Bonnie. "My mom will probably be home in an hour or so." She walked over to the window. "The storm still looks a ways away."

But the gray clouds were definitely there, Bonnie thought. And coming closer.

She hung up the telephone and went outside. The wind was getting stronger, she noticed. Her hair blew in her eyes as she closed and latched the storm shutters on the beach side of the house. She could still watch the water from her mother's study, where the window glass wasn't in danger from blowing sand and debris off the water.

Running back inside, she stuffed towels under the back door and latched the screen door securely. There was nothing to do now but wait.

She turned on the radio so she could listen for the weather report, and tried her mother's cell phone again. This time she got her voicemail.

"Mom! Call me as soon as you can! Pops VanGelderen thinks the storm coming in this afternoon is going to be a bad one. And I can see a bunch of dark clouds coming our way!"

Just then the weather report came on the radio, and Bonnie hung up the phone to go listen.

"The Weather Service has issued a severe storm and gale warning for the Rose, Bluewater, and Mermaid Islands for early afternoon. Residents are urged to stay inside and to take measures to prepare for severe weather conditions."

Her heart pounding, Bonnie ran to the window in her mother's study. The gray was growing darker, and seemed to be reaching with greedy fingers toward Mermaid Island. But scarier still was how the waves seemed to be tossing and swirling. It was as if they didn't know which direction to go. It was strange and frightening to watch; yet Bonnie felt an odd thrill run down her arms.

Were the waves dancing with the merpeople? Were they moving to music that only people of the water could hear?

Just then the phone rang, and Bonnie scrambled to answer.

It was Caro Campbell, sounding anxious.

"They say the storm is still several hours away, but I'm coming home now," she said. "The traffic here is terrible, and I don't want to miss the next ferry."

"Good!" answered Bonnie. "I've got things ready at the cabin, but I feel a lot better knowing you're coming back. I know you want your information from the Library, but ..."

"I'm coming home now," said Caro Campbell firmly. "You were right. I never should have gone this morning. " She sighed, then said, "I'd better go. There's a line of cars here, and I see a police officer up ahead. I think there may be a traffic light out."

Bonnie said goodbye to her mother, then wandered back into the study to keep an eye on the approaching storm. Out in the kitchen she could hear the radio announcer occasionally interrupt the music program with a weather update. The predictions were becoming more alarming. The storm that had been safely over the water appeared to have unexpectedly turned toward land, with Mermaid Island right in its path.

But Bonnie felt satisfied that she had done as the mermaid had directed. Her mother was on the way home, their little cabin was buttoned up tight and dry, the town-dwellers on the island were prepared, her friends at 2588 had left their shops secure...

Bonnie suddenly sat up straight in her chair, her eyes widening. Angie and Mrs. Caswell had both gone to the mainland last night, Angie to stay with her sister, Mrs. Caswell with Julie. And before she left, Angie had carefully prepared the BookBin in case of bad weather. But what about Wild Violets?

The storm shutters weren't closed!

Bonnie turned back to the window and stared out at the gathering clouds. Why, oh why, hadn't they closed them last night? Bonnie clenched her fists with frustration at her own carelessness.

She tried to telephone Moonie again, but the line was busy. Bobbie's line was busy as well.

Were the village phones working? Bonnie wondered.

She called her mother's cell phone and got her voicemail.

Frustrated, Bonnie thumped the phone back in its cradle. She looked out once more at the clouds, and then ran to grab her raincoat and the key to Wild Violets.

I'll run as fast as I can to the village, close up Wild Violets, then run straight back. There's time…there must be time! she thought, and felt goose bumps race over her arms. She didn't want to go out in the storm, but she couldn't let Wild Violets suffer another accident. If the front window got broken and storm caused a lot of damage, Mrs. Caswell might give up on her dream of having a store on Mermaid Island.

And if that happens, it will be my fault, Bonnie told herself bitterly.

She called her mother again and left a message on her voicemail telling her where she was going, then opened the door and ran out into the rising wind.

12

Panting, Bonnie pounded down the beach path, shading her eyes from blowing sand and leaves. The sky was a steely gray now, and waves churned angrily against the old log as Bonnie ran past, her sneakers sliding in the deep sand.

Nearly there, she thought anxiously. I'll be at the shop and home again in no time.

She fought her way through the tall grass at the edge of the beach, and then ran down the boardwalk to Wild Violets. Carefully, she pulled the string to Julie's bucket and heard the bracket drop into place.

Bonnie smiled grimly. No water on her head today! But she must remember to reset the trap before she left, she told herself.

Quickly, she pulled the storm shutters closed and fastened the latches, then ran inside the store and into Mrs. Caswell's office to check the window there.

She tried the lights, but nothing came on. The storm must have blown out the electricity, she thought.

It was then that she heard a key in the door.

"It's not locked!" she opened her mouth to call, then froze.

Who would be coming into Wild Violets with the storm approaching? It had to be Julie, but...Bonnie's heart began to pound.

Cautiously, she parted the curtain at the office door and peeked out. For a moment, she could see nothing in the gathering gloom from the storm. Then she made out the figure of a woman with her hair caught back in a braid.

Angie! gasped Bonnie, but then as the woman turned and Bonnie ducked back behind the curtain, Bonnie saw it was not Angie, but Ms. Reynolds, Fred Mahoney's assistant!

What is she doing here? And where did she get a key to Wild Violets? Bonnie thought with alarm.

Frightened, Bonnie slid deeper into the shadows in Mrs. Caswell's office.

The wind hit 2588 with a sudden howl, and Bonnie heard Ms. Reynolds begin to laugh.

"Perfect!" she cried. "What damage these island storms can do! It's such a shame about this store. Now, let's see. I think one of the shutters must have blown open…" Bonnie heard the sound of the latches unfastening on the shutters she had just so carefully closed.

"And look! The wind blew this down!" There was a crash, and Bonnie winced.

She tried to reach around the curtain for the phone, but it was too far away on the shop counter. She pulled her hand back and strained her ears, thinking frantically.

Out in the main part of the store Ms. Reynolds was striding around, muttering to herself.

"Such a shame that you didn't close the shop up before the storm!" Ms. Reynolds cried. "Now look what has happened! All your lovely things are ruined! Nothing to do but to move on! You're just an old lady, anyway. You can't run this shop on your own! And now you've had still another accident in your shop. Better close down before something worse happens!"

There was a thump and a piece of pottery shattered. Bonnie heard a table tip, and the sound of a heavy object sliding across the floor.

She had to do something! Ms. Reynolds was going to wreck Wild Violets!

Cautiously, Bonnie peeked out around the curtain again. When she saw Ms. Reynolds' back was to her, she crept out to the counter and crawled underneath it. Reaching up, she pulled the phone down and clutched it tightly in her hand.

Suddenly, the store went quiet, and Bonnie strained her ears to hear what was happening.

"Hello?" Ms. Reynolds' rather high-pitched voice called.

Ms. Reynolds took several steps toward the back of the store, and then stopped. She was listening, Bonnie thought. She had heard something! Bonnie held her hand over her mouth to try to silence her frightened breathing. Was there time to call 911? Was the telephone even working?

She felt sick to her stomach, and her heart was thumping so loudly that she was sure Ms. Reynolds could hear it out in the store.

"Is anyone there?!" Ms. Reynolds cried shrilly, and Bonnie heard her begin to walk toward the office.

A few more steps and she would be at the counter. Bonnie would be discovered!

Shaking with fear, she began pressing the buttons for 911. Then, to her horror, she heard the door to Wild Violets crash open again.

"Maria!" a man's voice bellowed, and over the screech of the wind Bonnie heard Ms. Reynolds gasp.

"What are you doing?!" shouted the new voice, and Bonnie heard someone stride into the shop, slamming the door.

"I…Wild Violets…the lease…" Ms. Reynolds stammered, and then she cried, "Fred, I was doing what I thought best for you, for your business!"

"Best for me!" shouted the second voice, and Bonnie put her shaking hands over her ears.

It was Mr. Mahoney, and by the sound of it, he was furious at Ms. Reynolds.

"You're fired!" Mr. Mahoney yelled. "I wondered if you weren't up to something when Polly VanGelderen told me this store had been having strange accidents! I made a fair and square offer for the 2588 building, but if they won't sell, they won't sell! I've lived on Mermaid Island since I was a boy, and these people are my neighbors! I never wanted you to do anything like this! Get off this island by morning, or I'll call the police on you. And give me that key!"

Rising up on her cramped legs, Bonnie peeked over the counter to see Mr. Mahoney tugging Ms. Reynolds toward the door.

She struggled away from him. "Fred, I'm nearly sure there's someone in here," she cried, and Mr. Mahoney turned to look over his shoulder.

Bonnie ducked. Oh no! she thought frantically.

She pressed herself as tightly as she could against the counter and prayed. But Mr. Mahoney wouldn't hurt her, would he? Would he?!

There was a short silence, and then she heard Fred Mahoney's growl, "It would serve us both right if someone saw us. I've been a horrible fool."

He rushed Ms. Reynolds the rest of the way to the door.

Ms. Reynolds was arguing and pleading with him, but Mr. Mahoney ignored her and prodded her out ahead of him into the wind. He stopped to re-fasten the shutters over the big window, and then Bonnie heard their footsteps hurrying away down the boardwalk.

Bonnie stood up and looked around, breathing hard. It had been Ms. Reynolds all along who had been causing the accidents in Wild Violets!

She set the telephone back on the counter. What would have happened if Mr. Mahoney had arrived just a few minutes later? Ms. Reynolds might have found her hiding place! What would she have done?

Gulping, Bonnie started for the door, stepping around a toppled table, and looking sorrowfully at a broken plate.

There was nothing she could do about the mess right now, she told herself. Several pieces of Mrs. Caswell's lovely artwork had been ruined, and sand and a few sticks had blown in through the open door, but nothing had happened that could not be repaired tomorrow.

It was time for Bonnie to leave. The storm was coming and quickly. She must get home right away.

She was reaching for the door handle when, to her shock, she heard more footsteps running up the boardwalk.

Bonnie dove for the counter and wedged herself behind it just as the door flew still again. At the same time the sky outside opened and rain hit the island with a roar, blowing into the shop and sending papers cascading down onto Bonnie's head.

Crouched shuddering in her hiding place, Bonnie was sure this time she going to faint from fear when she heard Caro Campbell's frightened voice cry, "Bonnie! Bonnie! Are you here?!" and Bonnie scrambled out into her mother's arms.

13

For a few moments, mother and daughter stood hugging each other, laughing and crying as the rain poured down, soaking their clothing and streaming into their eyes.

"I was so worried when I got your voicemail!" Caro Campbell cried.

"The most terrible thing happened..." Bonnie gasped at the same time.

Caro Campbell pulled Bonnie inside Wild Violets, slammed the door closed and stood panting, holding Bonnie tightly in her arms.

Then her mother looked around the store. "What on earth?" she gasped, staring at the pieces of broken china on the floor.

So Bonnie began to tell the story, her words tumbling over each other. By now, she had to shout to be heard over the howl of the wind and crashes of thunder.

"It was Ms. Reynolds, Mom! Ms. Reynolds was trying to drive Mrs. Caswell out and get her to close Wild Violets! And she probably would have wrecked Angie's store, too, except..."

Something blew with a crash against the wall outside, and Bonnie jumped violently. Peeking through the little window in the shop door, Caro Campbell shook her head and then turned to her frightened daughter.

"We've got to get out of here, Bonnie," she cried. "If we can get to the car, I think I can still drive us home!"

"But the wind, Mom..." Bonnie began, and saw her mother glance with worried eyes out toward the water.

"I know," she said quietly. "But I think we should chance it. This old house...It's like a hurricane out there! And it's going to get worse, I'm afraid."

"It'll be safe here, Mom!" exclaimed Bonnie. "Millicent Proctor built her house to withstand the storms. Bobbie and Moonie's granddad said so. We can wait here in Wild Violets!"

"Oh, Bonnie," cried her mother. "There's no radio and no electricity here!"

"We've got a radio," answered Bonnie, and ran for the office. She held out the little portable she had stored there for Mrs. Caswell. "There's a flashlight and a couple of containers of water, too!" said Bonnie proudly.

Caro Campbell gazed at her worriedly. "Well, at least we have emergency supplies. It's not safe to drive home, I know, but...Okay, let's wait the storm out here. I just hope this old house doesn't come down around our ears!"

As the storm raged outside, the Campbells pulled two chairs out of the office, shook the rain off their jackets, and then huddled close together by the counter. The wind roared around 2588, rattling the shutters and shaking the roof. Lightning shot again and again across the sky.

Bonnie turned on the radio and mother and daughter strained their ears to hear above the roar of the wind.

"...Severe storm system shaking Mermaid and Bluewater Islands," said the radio announcer, as rain and hail pounded against the walls. "Record breaking weather, bringing high winds and rough waters."

"I wonder how Bobbie and Moonie are doing," Bonnie said anxiously.

Through the little window in the door, she could see that the sky had turned a murky green, one moment sullen and silent, then erupting in angry thunder and lightning.

"If they're doing anywhere near as well as we are, then they're just fine," answered Bonnie's mother. Then she added. "You were right. This old place seems well able to handle the storm."

Bonnie nodded and settled back in her chair, wrapping her arms around her bent knees. Despite the shriek of the wind and the pounding rain, Bonnie felt a curious feeling of comfort. Snuggled here in Wild Violets was like being inside a bubble of warmth and safety, as if...

And then she heard it.

A soft crooning on the wind. A humming, not quite a song, not quite a chant, yet the sound had a curious melody that seemed to be coming from the middle of the storm itself...rising joyfully and then dying away, only to swell again on the next gust of wind.

Bonnie's skin began to prickle. It was the sounds she had heard twice before, and the voices sounded musical and sweet.

And now Bonnie knew what it was! The merpeople were nearby, and they were singing and laughing. Bonnie was hearing their celebration!

She sat straight up in her chair and stared at the window, then glanced over at her mother. But Caro Campbell's eyes had begun to droop closed. She yawned and stretched.

"I feel odd," she murmured to Bonnie, and yawned again. "So sleepy. How can I feel sleepy with the wind howling around like this?"

She leaned back in her chair, resting her head against the cushion. "Do you care if I doze a little?" she asked Bonnie at last. "I just can't seem to keep my eyes open!"

Bonnie shook her head and watched as her mother curled deeper into the chair, pillowing her head on her arm. Soon she was breathing slowly and evenly, caught in the spell of the mermaid...deeply asleep and dreaming.

Bonnie rose quietly and laid her jacket over her mother's shoulders, then flipped off the radio and tiptoed to the door. Squinting, she peered through the streaming window out at the water.

At first she could see nothing through the wind and blowing sand, but then she realized to her astonishment that the world outside Wild Violets was whirling in a kind of wild dance. Trees bowed toward, then away from the water, and the tall grass Bonnie had run through so often flattened, stirred, then tossed back the other way like the long blowing hair of a woman.

Beyond the sand, the waves rose in tall peaks, tossed their white caps toward the swirling clouds, and then threw themselves against the shore, reaching nearly to the boardwalk before retreating, only to start all over again.

Bonnie thought suddenly of Millicent Proctor and how she had gazed out at the storms approaching Mermaid Island from her porch in this old house so many years ago. If Mrs. Proctor were here, she might be standing where Bonnie was now...watching and listening while the storm blew across the water.

Bonnie's eyes widened. Out in the water, a light moved. Then another blinked, shone palely, and disappeared. Purple, turquoise, and golden, the tiny lights glittered in the waves, then flickered out and appeared again, circling and dipping.

A deep bronze glow spread under the surface of the water.

Bonnie closed her eyes for a moment and felt a coolness on her eyelids, touching gently and then flowing past. Something very odd was happening, but she was not afraid. Instead, she felt filled with excitement.

Her mother made a gentle sound in her sleep and Bonnie glanced over at her. Caro Campbell was smiling softly, as if lost in a beautiful dream, but Bonnie's vision suddenly seemed hazy and rippled. Her mother appeared to be sitting far away, in some other place.

Slowly, Bonnie turned her gaze back to the water. She felt as if her bones had melted, that her body could bend and turn, weightless, in a thousand different directions. Shadowy figures seem to circle and whirl around her in the darkened room.

Then, to her astonishment, on the horizon Bonnie saw hundreds of arms reaching up out of the waves toward the sky. Hands open and outstretched, the people of the water caught the nourishing rain that poured down out of the clouds.

The dance went on and on, beautiful and strange, and Bonnie felt it all, saw it all, as if she were there with the mermaid and her people out in the water.

The sounds of the celebration filled her ears, drowning out the thunder, drowning out the rain crashing against the roof, drowning out even the pounding of the waves, so that Bonnie could hear nothing but the glad sounds of the merpeople's music.   She closed her eyes.

The storm whirled around the old house, and the wind blew on and on, but Bonnie did not notice time passing.   All she could feel was the joy of the merpeople as they welcomed the rain and celebrated the new life in the water.

Then it was over.   The gusts striking the old house began to lessen, and the downpour died away to a steady drizzle.   The music drifted away on the wind, and soon it was lost in the steady pulse of the surf.

Nothing remained of the colors in the water but drifts of bronze and touches of pink under a gradually lightening sky.   Sadly, Bonnie felt the room begin to return to normal.

The air ceased to ripple. The gliding coolness she had felt over her skin was gone.

Caro Campbell's eyes slowly opened and she gazed around her as if she had forgotten where they were.

"Wow!" she exclaimed, stretching and rubbing her eyes. "I was really asleep. And such dreams! For a minute I thought..." she stopped. "Oh never mind," she said.

"The storm seems to be passing," Bonnie said quietly.

Her mother strode over to the door and peeked out, then glanced down at her watch.

"It's been hours!" she exclaimed. "How on earth....? We'd better get home!"

Hours? Bonnie thought in amazement. It seemed like just a few moments ago when she and her mother had come for shelter into Wild Violets!

The Campbells put Wild Violets back in order, sweeping up the china Maria Reynolds had broken. Then they gathered up their belongings and dashed through light rain out to the car, dodging branches and a lawn chair that had blown into the parking lot.

"Looks like a few trees down!" commented Bonnie's mother. "I hope my beech grove on the west side is okay!"

They drove home in silence, gazing out at piles of twigs and blown debris, and a broken telephone wire. In one spot, the gravel road that led to the cabin was washed away so badly that Caro Campbell almost got the car stuck.

But soon they reached their little home on the beach and let themselves thankfully inside. It was dry and warm, and the electricity flickered on a few minutes later, so Caro Campbell made herself a cup of coffee and went to inspect the outside of the house.

"Some wind damage here!" she called. "Something hit the house...maybe a branch or something. And here's a broken shutter!"

Bonnie phoned Moonie and Bobbie to make sure their families were all right, then went upstairs to her room and lay down on her bed.

If she and her mother had come home to the cabin, would she have been able join the mermaid during her celebration? 2588 was a very special place, and perhaps it *did* have a kind of magic after all. Mrs. Proctor must have known it. Was that why she had loved the storms so much?

But something had happened today that Bonnie had thought could never be. For a few precious hours, she had felt herself a part of the mermaid's world under the water...something she had dreamed of doing all summer. Bonnie touched her necklace and felt her grandmother's pearl, warm and soft under her fingers.

14

The Mermaid Island residents cleaned up, repaired and talked endlessly about the big storm. Where had the wind been the strongest, which had been the biggest bolt of lightning?

Bonnie listened and smiled, then sat at the beach for hours on driftwood scrubbed nearly white by the wind and sand, watching the water. Sometimes she wandered through the tall grass and remembered how it had swayed and danced in the gusting wind.

The mermaid came to the old log, and Bonnie sat with her for an entire evening, talking and laughing, telling stories and remembering.

Mermaid Dreams

"Have your people gone home?" Bonnie asked, thinking of the hands she had seen stretching up toward the sky out of the waves.

The mermaid was quiet for a moment. Then she said, "Yes, most are gone away now. But because of the celebration, there will be more of us here. We are of the water, and now the water is new and young. I think you will notice it is different, even for you."

Bonnie glanced down the beach. "Different?" she asked. "Different for me? How?"

The mermaid stirred and Bonnie saw her turquoise tail gleam under the water. "During the celebration you were very close to us," she answered in her odd, rushing voice. "You have returned to your own world, but there is...an opening now. Perhaps you will see it."

Bonnie jumped to her feet. "An opening?! Like a window? To you?"

"A window," answered the mermaid quietly. "Perhaps."

Bonnie creased her brow. There was so much she did not know or understand about the mermaid and her people. But maybe now there was a chance to learn. She sat back down on the log and gazed at the beautiful creature in the water, glowing since the big storm with a new light, a new brilliance.

"An opening," she whispered. "I like that."

The mermaid smiled.

The sky began to darken, and Bonnie said farewell. Walking along the beach toward home under the early stars, she looked out at the Mermaid Island waves.

Were the mermaid and her people watching? It gave Bonnie a comforting feeling, as if she were surrounded by a circle of warmth. Ahead, she could see the lights of the cabin glowing gently. Inside, her mother would be reading or working at her computer. Perhaps they would have a cup of hot chocolate together and share a few stories of their own about the storm before heading off to bed.

But the biggest story of all was of Bonnie's secret visit with the people under the water, and that was a tale she would never tell.

Wild Violets opened to the public, and it was busy with visitors admiring Mrs. Caswell's beautiful china. Mrs. Caswell sold a twelve-piece setting of dishes and two little tables on the very first day. She was excited and happy about her success.

Fred Mahoney visited the store on its opening day, but Ms. Reynolds was not with him. He had spread the word that she left Mermaid Island rather suddenly...probably scared off by the storm.

Bonnie and her mother had explained to Mrs. Caswell and Julie about the incident during the storm, but they told no one else. In the end, Mr. Mahoney had stopped Maria Reynolds from doing much damage in the store, and Mrs. Caswell and Julie were satisfied that there would be no more "accidents" in Wild Violets.

Polly VanGelderen mentioned that Mr. Mahoney was interested in renovating another old house farther down the beach, and might turn it into a duplex. He seemed now to have a new interest in preserving old buildings, and had withdrawn his offer to buy 2588. The Historical Committee celebrated with frollops for everyone in 2588, even Carlotta Anastasia.

Next, Angie had her grand opening, and the BookBin featured a visit by a local author who had written a storybook about mermaids. Bonnie bought an autographed copy and set it on the shelf by her jewelry case.

Two more shops began to move into the 2588 building, and soon the old house was bustling with activity. Carpenters restored the wood in the oaken staircase, people hurried in and out carrying boxes and cleaning supplies, and customers wandered along the boardwalk, sipping frollops and admiring items in the new shops.

All in all, it was a satisfactory end to an exciting summer, Bonnie thought, as she shut the book she was reading and leaned back in her chair on the boardwalk. She closed her eyes and let the Mermaid Island sunshine warm her face. Out in the water somewhere, perhaps the mermaid was resting just as Bonnie was right now, enjoying a moment in the warm wind.

Bonnie heard voices, and she looked up to see Bobbie and Moonie approaching. Moonie was leading Carlotta Anastasia on her leash, and the cousins were arguing good-naturedly.

"No, Angie didn't say that," Bobbie insisted. "She *said* the travel books were going to go by the window and be the featured section for the week."

"She said they would go by the window," replied Moonie. "But in the white case. The display case doesn't have room in it."

"No, she didn't!" countered Bobbie.

Moonie stopped suddenly. "We can ask her in a minute. Let's go into Wild Violets."

"Why?" demanded Bobbie. "Mrs. Caswell just left for a lunch break."

"Come on!" answered Moonie. "I want to show you something."

"Oh, okay," answered Bobbie rather grumpily, reaching for the knob and pulling the door open. "But just for a min....eeeek!"

Bonnie jumped to her feet at Bobbie's shriek, and turned to see her friend standing, fists clenched, with Julie's water bucket upside down on her head. Spluttering and coughing and shaking her soaking wet hair, Bobbie pulled the bucket off and turned furiously toward Moonie, who was bent double laughing.

"You did that on purpose!" Bobbie shouted at her cousin, and waved the bucket at Moonie. "There's a little bit left!" she threatened, and Moonie took off at a run with Carlotta Anastasia scampering alongside her, barking merrily.

Bobbie followed in hot pursuit, flinging diamond drops of water that twinkled in the Mermaid Island sunlight.

Angie emerged from the BookBin and stood, hands on her hips, staring after the fleeing girls.

"What was that all about?" she asked Bonnie, and began to laugh.

Then she jumped and, shading her eyes with her hand, stared intently out at the water.

"Did you see that?!" she exclaimed.

Bonnie turned to look.

"What?" she asked.

Angie stood stiffly for a moment, and then her shoulders relaxed.

"Oh, it's just a boat," she said. "Never mind."

Bonnie joined Angie at the railing and looked out at the water. The wind lifted her hair gently, teasing it along her cheek, and the bright sunshine turned the tossing waves into a glittering sheet of light.

Angie sighed and looked over at Bonnie with a faint smile. "Do you ever think there is something slightly magical about Mermaid Island?" she asked at last.

Bonnie grinned at her. "I do," she answered. "I really, really do."

Beneath the Waves

I am the waves,
I am the life,
I am the ocean.
The fish are my friends and the whale is my brother.
He sings to me.
The seaweed is my hair,
The sunshine is my fingernails.
My eyes are pearls from the sea's largest oyster.
My tail is the water,
My life is the ocean.
All of them talk to me and yet they do not make a
sound.
I am a creature of the sea.
I am the mermaid.

- Sally McBurgundy

Nature's Mermaids

Did you know that there are creatures living right here in the United States that sailors  may once have mistaken for mermaids? They're manatees...gentle, slow-moving mammals that eat submerged and floating grass and communicate with other manatees through chirps, whistles or squeaks.

Sadly, manatees are an endangered species, partly because they can easily be injured or killed by propellers on motorized boats.

Manatees could use your help. There are several organizations that are dedicated to helping save the manatee. You can find out more information on the Internet about the manatee by visiting:

http://www.savethemanatee.org

Did you miss the any of the other Mermaid Island books?

In <u>The Secret of Mermaid Island</u>, Bonnie meets her friends, Bobbie and Moonie, and discovers Mermaid Island's special secret.

In <u>The Mermaid's Gift</u>, divers seeking a long-lost shipwreck threaten the secret Bonnie has tried so hard to protect.

Mermaid Island books are available by sending a check to:

Riley Press
P.O. Box 202
Eagle, MI 48822

Cost: $7.25/book
(includes shipping and handling)

You may also order online from the Riley Press website. Please visit
http://rileypress.hypermart.net

About the Author

Judith Wade lives in Michigan with her family, including her husband and daughter, dogs, cats, guinea pigs, fish and an ex-racehorse.

She loves to ride horseback, do stained glass, play in her garden and, of course, write.

Yes, one of her dogs is a pug. You may email Judith Wade at: *jwadewrites@yahoo.com*